❋ *PARTIES* ❋

CARL VAN VECHTEN

PARTIES

Scenes from Contemporary

New York Life

SUN &
MOON

CLASSICS

31

Sun & Moon Press
A Program of The Contemporary Arts Educational Project, Inc.
a nonprofit corporation
6026 Wilshire Boulevard, Los Angeles, California 90036

This edition first published in paperback in 1993 by Sun & Moon Press
10 9 8 7 6 5 4 3 2 1
FIRST SUN & MOON EDITION
©Carl Van Vechten, 1930
Reprinted by permission of Alfred A. Knopf publishers
Biographical information © Sun & Moon Press, 1993
All rights reserved

This book was made possible, in part, through a grant from the
Andrew W. Mellon Foundation, the National Endowment for the Arts,
and through contributions to The Contemporary Arts
Educational Project, Inc. a nonprofit corporation

Cover: Romare Bearden,
Wrapping It up at the Lafayette
The Cleveland Museum of Art,
Mr. & Mrs. William H. Martlatt Fund
© Estate of Romare Bearden
Design: Katie Messborn

LIBRARY OF CONGRESS CATALOGING IN PUBLICATION DATA
Van Vechten, Carl
Parties
p. cm. — (Sun & Moon Classics: 31)
ISBN: 1-55713-029-9
I. Title. II. Series.
811'.54—dc20

Printed in the United States of America on acid-free paper

This book is dedicated with deep affection

to

Armina Marshall

and

Lawrence Langner

who have gone to many parties

with me

"*Ce n'est pas dans la nouveauté, c'est dans l'habitude que nous trouvons les plus grands plaisirs.*"

RAYMOND RADIGUET

⁂ *ONE* ⁂

Hamish Wilding was very drunk at the time, but he never afterwards forgot the distorted figure of David Westlake as he appeared to him, hatless, his hair mussed, in the bar of the Harlem speakeasy where they had agreed to meet. There was blood on David's lips as they opened to cry: I've killed a man or a man has killed me. There were three of us on the stairs. I mean . . . O God!

Before he should divulge more information of an incriminating nature to the inquisitive group that lounged about the bar, Hamish dragged his friend outside and more or less hurled him into the maw of a taxi fortuitously waiting at the kerb.

As they drove down Seventh Avenue and through the Park David continued to mumble his strange story: Three of us on the stairs, I tell you. We wanted to go in.

Where was this? Hamish angled for a clue.

I mean . . . O God! In the bowels of the earth. Climbing, always climbing. . . . Nearer my God to thee

and Go down Moses! Well, I sat on the fellow's chest and pummelled him and the stars began to fall. Chunks of dirt in his hair bit my hands. Then we dropped. We musta tumbled in a well. There was water. I died first.

The relaxed muscles in David's neck permitted his head to rest on Hamish's shoulder.

Where were you? Hamish persisted quietly.

In a mountain. The girl . . .

What girl?

took us there. She was dressed in pink and played the mandolin. The waiter said she had psittacosis. You woulda liked her. I did. We played a fine game of basketball and I came right through. Then she went to the dentist and the romp began on the stairs. If the police hadn't come . . .

You haven't been arrested?

Sure, you hound. There you have the story.

The Park lights flickered uncertainly. David fell asleep, his head resting on Hamish's shoulder. Hamish drunkenly tried to put three and four together. There had been, he was aware from David's condition, a fight. Well, bed would probably straighten everything out. They both needed sleep: so much was certain. Hamish, too, yielded to his drowsiness and knew nothing more until he was awakened by a persistent din which continued long after he had opened his eyes and stretched forth a naked arm. Eventually he contrived to lift the receiver.

Hello, he sleepily challenged the transmitter.

Hamish . . . the poignancy of the voice brought him immediately to his senses . . . Hamish, I've killed myself.

How?

Not jumped out of an airplane like that silly girl, or bumped myself off in a hop-joint, or drowned myself, or taken cyanide . . .

What *have* you done, Rilda? Hamish's tone was agonized.

Never you mind, Hamish. You guess.

Where are you?

You guess.

What's the matter? Why have you done this, Rilda?

David's sailed for Paris with that Fern boy.

The connection was broken.

[handwritten margin note: Set up of queer coupling in fantasy]

Replacing the receiver, Hamish turned to discover David snoring at his elbow. David asleep this very early morning was not too pretty a sight. The blood had caked on his lip, his face and hands were dirty, his black, curly hair matted and untidy. Unaccountably here he was lying in Hamish's bed, quite naked, and Rilda believed he had sailed for Europe with . . .

Hamish shook his guest roughly.

Hey! Rilda has killed herself.

David opened one eye and groaned.

Your wife's killed herself.

Who? David muttered interrogatively.

Rilda.

Where?

Wake up, you louse. I don't know where.

David raised his head. What did you say about Rilda? he demanded.

She's killed herself.

How do you know? She's got a helluva nerve telling you before she tells me. Anyway, I don't believe it. She's drunk.

She says she did it because you've gone to Paris with that Fern boy.

Now I know she's drunk. How do you suppose she got hold of that?

Who is the Fern boy?

That fine little rotter who works in Donald's speakeasy. You know him. He's always drunk. I told him I'd take him to Paris sometime. Maybe I will.

David, I say, did you really kill a man last night?

David's blue eyes expressed their owner's astonishment.

Are you drunk, too? he demanded. I dined with Rosalie Keith last night and took you home afterwards. You got drunk and insulted Rosalie on the stairs. So I dragged you out. Lovely old thing, Rosalie.

How did you hurt your lip?

Does my lip hurt? David touched it with his forefinger

4

and chuckled. Biting chunks out of Rosalie's champagne glasses probably, he suggested.

Hamish's tone became a shade more serious: David, you met me in the Plum Pudding last night and said you had dropped somebody down a well.

You're certainly drunk, Hamish.

Thrusting one leg out of bed and following it with the other, David pushed his hands through his tousled curls and rising unsteadily, crossed the floor to observe himself in the mirror. Recoiling from the unflattering reflection in mock horror, he laughed a little and then shuddered.

By God, I *do* remember something, he exclaimed, something very messy and noisy and bumpy. There must have been a saxophone at the bottom of that well. What were you saying about Fern?

The conversation was interrupted by the telephone bell.

Hello, Hamish, sitting on the edge of the bed, replied.

Say, that you, Hamish? This is Donald Bliss.

Didn't know bootleggers rose so early.

Don't try to be funny. I ain't been to bed. Do you know where David is?

Sure. I can find him.

Well, tell him Roy Fern's dead. Bumped off in some Harlem speakeasy last night. They found him on the street.

Where is he now?

I dunno. I just got the police call. They knew he worked for me. I dunno. I didn't ask.

The sound of the clicking receiver came over the wire to Hamish.

Great God, man . . . Hamish turned to his friend who had slumped back into bed . . . that was Donald, Donald Bliss. He says Roy Fern was bumped off in a speakeasy last night.

O Jeese! A moan burst from David's lips. I loved that boy. A fine little rotter he was, too. O Jeese! Say, Hame, I gotta have a drink.

Hamish consulted the vermilion lacquer cabinet near his bed.

There's a coupla drops of Pernod here and some Martell, he announced.

Well, mix 'em. I ain't got any nerve left. Poor Fern. Say, I promised to take that kid to Paris.

With an unsteady hand Hamish poured brandy into a tall glass until it was half full and then added Pernod until the glass was brimming. Sitting up in bed, David gulped down this mixture.

Better order a coupla sidecars, he advised. We gotta have a drink. Poor little Roy is dead. Poor little kid.

Hamish drew a dressing-gown of mustard and white striped silk around David's shoulders. Rilda is dead too, he reminded David, a little reproachfully, but he rang the bell.

So she is. Poor Rilda. He sighed and said to Hamish's man who appeared at the door, Give us a coupla sidecars, Boker. Probably Irene's dead too, he added, if you only knowed.

There's music to that, Hamish commented.

I know, David replied impatiently.

Sidecars taste good after brandy, Hamish remarked, emptying the remaining contents of the Martell bottle into a glass which he raised to his own lips.

Nothing like Pernod to put you on your feet, David responded.

What are you going to do? Hamish demanded.

Nothing. Why? About what?

About Rilda and Roy Fern.

I'll tell you . . . I mean it's getting serious. Something's gotta be done. I gotta lead an entirely new life. Hame, I gotta get some new friends.

David was sobbing softly.

Yes, but aren't you going to call Rilda up?

Who?

Rilda.

She's dead. Rilda's dead. How can I call her up?

You don't even know how she killed herself or where she is.

O Jeese! She got bumped off in a Harlem speakeasy and they found her on the street. I know the whole goddam racket.

The telephone bell rang.

Hamish managed a feeble Hello.

A firm voice inquired, Is David with you?

I think so.

Well, did you tell him I'd killed myself?

Certainly not. I don't want to upset him.

Well, I didn't kill myself. The Fern boy's dead and so now we're quits.

Hamish listened vainly for more. The voice apparently had no further information to vouchsafe.

That was Rilda again, he explained to David.

Yeah? David responded without much interest.

Boker entered bearing a tray containing two highball glasses full of sidecars. He left with orders for two more.

What does she want? David inquired after a pause.

I don't know. She was talking about Fern.

Poor Fern! He's dead. Nice, little kid, Roy. . . David essayed once more to stagger across the floor to the dressing-table where he might examine himself in the mirror. Deciding to properly put on the dressing-gown, he found some difficulty in coping with the sleeves. . . By God, Hame, he cried, as his left arm at last shot through the correct hole, I'm sorry I killed him.

Hamish, who had been reclining, sat bolt upright in bed.

You didn't kill him, David!

I most certainly did, that one replied tranquilly and with great dignity. I certainly killed him.

At this juncture Boker entered with a new supply of cocktails, fortifying his masters against their immediate future with a two quart shakerful.

Boker, I killed a man last night, David insisted.

Yes sir. Boker barely lifted his eyebrows.

I killed a man. Going to get ten years for it.

Thank you, sir. David staggered back to bed as Boker bowed himself out.

I'll bet Boker's the only sober man in this block, David complained as he put his arm affectionately around Hamish's shoulder.

Hamish felt both horrified and bewildered.

Do you know what you've just said, David? he demanded. Why, you're a confessed murderer.

Sure, I killed him. I murdered poor little Fern. . . David began to cry again. . . I murdered him on the staircase at Rosalie Keith's. She hit me over the head with a champagne bottle, the bitch, he muttered savagely. You don't know about Rosalie. Well, I do. *That* one! he hinted darkly.

What are you going to do, David? Hamish was all concern for his friend now.

Take another drink, I suppose.

About Fern?

Oh, poor kid. I killed him. I set the corpse afire and it

burned like one of those fiery crosses of the Ku Klux. Then I tied him to the back of my taxi and dragged him four miles through the ice and snow to where his body was discovered in Yonkers, half eaten by water-rats and bears. It had been there for eight days.

You fool! He was killed last night.

I oughta know when I killed him. I guess I do too. Rosalie's teeth are false, her legs are false, and so's her champagne and her jewelry. I killed him, I tell you, in a Harlem speakeasy. There were three of us and a woman in blue, with who, with *whom* I was playing tennis in Van Cortlandt Park after I left that Keith bitch. No wonder I cut my lip and my wisdom teeth. There was a helluva scrap on the stairs and then I felt myself falling, falling, falling . . . I mean like London Bridge or the Tower of Pisa or Niagara or rain. Fern was a good boy, a fine little rotter. On the make, but all right. I'm glad I killed him.

You swine, you dear old filthy swine! Hamish cried hysterically, hurling the contents of his glass at David, but they did not damage him, splashing over his head instead, slightly defacing an unframed lithograph by Marie Laurencin. Lifting one hand in silent deprecation, David laid his head gently on the pillow and extended his naked legs beneath the sheets. In an incredibly short time he had fallen asleep.

Hamish decided to take a bath and go to the club for a drink.

✳ *TWO* ✳

The Gräfin Adele von Pulmernl und Stilzernl was behaving most obstinately this evening. The sexagenarian (at the very least) kicked her small feet petulantly backwards and forwards while Fräulein Stupforsch made a vain attempt to draw on her high boots.

Nein, nein, the Gräfin, who was actually on strike, protested.

Her visit to America had been the execution of her own idea. She had believed it would prove an excellent antidote to the continual round of cures to which the aging German nobility had been consigned since the signing of the Armistice. The Gräfin had begun to feel that another season at Marienbad, Baden-Baden, or Karlsbad would be the end of her. She was thoroughly sick of the Grand Hotel Pupp. Nor did the Waldlust Hotel at Freudenstadt in the Schwarzwald or the Grand Hôtel de l'Europe at Salzburg delight her more. She was so well acquainted with the menus of the Walterspiel in München that she might have cooked them all herself and the mere thought of Frau Sacher sitting in front of her famous hotel in Wien reduced her to frenzy.

Born in Hanover, she had originally intended to become a concert pianist, a career almost equivalent to suicide in those far-off days. Instead she had married the Graf von Pulmernl und Stilzernl with his comic Saxon accent. Her sense of humour had encouraged her to put up with this and a great deal more. In the end, however, she did not even laugh at the idea of the servant whose sole occupation was to repeat the coloured sand replica of the family coat-of-arms before the door of the wine cellar each time the steward's feet had trampled it out.

She had outlived her generation: that was the difficulty. She had outlived two or three generations. The only persons who could actually cope with her superb vitality appeared to be the young Americans who sometimes unaccountably strayed into those tiresome watering-places to which her age, her position, and the attitude of her servants seemed endlessly to sentence her. Fräulein Stupforsch had been more to blame in this matter than anybody else. Fräulein Stupforsch had ordered her about in the most shocking manner. To be sure, Fräulein Stupforsch was more than a servant, but still, she, the Gräfin, should not have permitted her to fall into the habit of exercising so much authority. The fact was, the Gräfin had begun to realize, she had slipped into a rut in which it was simpler for her to let others determine the course of her life than to exert herself to assume the initiative.

She had, to be sure, long since found it expedient to close her dull Schloss in Silesia. It had become, she discovered, increasingly difficult for a sprightly (without exag-

geration) lady of seventy (or over) to surround herself
with desirable guests in an old castle in which the toilet
facilities were mediæval, and could scarcely be improved
upon without enormous expense, and in which the
draughts, owing to the great windows and wide fireplace
openings, were excessive. Moreover the Schloss von Pulmernl und Stilzernl was very nearly inaccessible, and arriving guests were further discouraged, when they actually
reached it after a tiresome motor-drive, by the impression
of despair conveyed by the wind whistling in a most melancholy manner through the fir-trees which hemmed in
the castle on every side. The result of these unfortunate
conditions was that the guest-chambers were usually occupied by extremely dull nieces and nephews who dressed
dowdily and conversed in frightened whispers. They ate
very heartily and occasionally shot pheasants or a game-
keeper. It is really no wonder that eventually, at the age of
seventy (or thereabouts), the Gräfin had turned over the
Schloss, furnished in the most overbearing amount of purple plush and containing so many paintings by Hans
Makart, especially the enormous canvas in the dining-
room representing Thusnelda in the triumphant procession
of Germanicus, that some of the Gräfin's more cynical acquaintances had dubbed the place the Schloss Makart, to
her poor spinster and bachelor relatives that they might
sit and grow old before their time, well-fed on the pheas-
ant and wild-boar that swarmed in the forest, by the trout

that shimmered in the mountain-streams, and by the red
cabbage and kohlrabi that grew in abundance in the garden.

The Gräfin found her residence in Dresden equally dull,
perhaps even more dull. She had long since come to the
conclusion that if there was one amusing person in this
Saxon city she had not encountered him or her, although
her facilities for forming acquaintanceships were practically unlimited. Her position made it essential, if she in-
habited this house during the season, that she should give
at least one large reception and several small dinners. Fur-
thermore, no one, who enjoyed the privilege of knowing
her, thought of arranging any formal affair while she was
in town without soliciting her participation. These people
considered they were doing her honour in inviting her
friends to meet her, but honour is not always pleasure, and
the Gräfin often reflected that she might be happier in
mixed company.

In the end she made a resolution. Announcing on her
departure that she would return as usual the following
year, she had caused the windows to be boarded up and
burglar-alarms communicating with a police-station added
to the further protection of the house. As Gräfin Adele von
Pulmernl und Stilzernl she had not quite been able to sum-
mon the courage to inform her friends that she intended
to shake the Dresden soil off her garment-hems for all
time, but that, nevertheless, was her intention. Later,
whenever she recalled the darkening Lenbach portrait of

the Count in full military uniform hanging over the mantelpiece in the drawing-room, or all those Frans Snyders paintings of dead animals and live fruit which concealed the greater part of the red damask on the walls of the dining-room, or the the gold chairs in the ball-room upholstered in red and black needle-point with the arms of Pulmernl und Stilzernl pricked therein, it gave her intense pleasure to realize that they were slowly disintegrating and that in any case she would never see them again.

This matter of lopping off estates and possessions had been easier to manage than she had foreseen. Fräulein Stupforsch had interposed a few feeble objections, to be sure, but she had not actually intervened to prevent the Gräfin from executing her projects. The difficulties had arisen after she had disposed of the Schloss and closed the Dresden house for what she was pleased to call an indefinite period. Her personal maid, Maria, who had been with her for forty years, was ignorant of all languages but German. Fräulein Stupforsch spoke a little halting French, but was incapable of following a conversation in that tongue. Her English, perhaps, was even less fluent. Now Maria, like Fräulein Stupforsch, through long association with the Gräfin had acquired the habit of making decisions for her. This was, of course, the fault of the Gräfin herself who liked, on most occasions, as so many people do, to have tiresome trifles settled for her. It gave her an added sense of protection and in German watering-places it relieved her of a great deal of responsibility, which in the circumstances she was delighted to be rid of. Besides, there is no doubt but that apathy to what was going on around her gave this attitude of her servants, who certainly were never insolent, an air of unimportance. However, after she had disposed of her houses and determined to see life and enjoy herself, she found it difficult to alter the conduct of her maid and companion. She could not very well travel without them and they flatly refused to escort her (as they put it, they would not permit her to go) to Paris or, indeed, to any locality whatever where they themselves would not feel completely at home. So they carried her along, always pouting and protesting prettily, her visage chronically screwed into a thousand wrinkles of dismay, from one dusty cure to another, from one provincial hotel to the next one. Her career in the past had not trained her to rebel, nor did she for a considerable period encounter a proper abetter, a suitable conspirator, to aid her in casting off the shackles of her tradition.

One afternoon, however, ensconced among the roses of a tea-garden at Karlsbad, drinking her tea in a kind of resignation, her short legs not permitting her booted feet to reach the sward, so that they dangled under her black taffeta dress an inch or two above the ground, the thing happened. She was quite alone. Fräulein Stupforsch had deserted her to visit the principal shopping street on some errand or other. How it had occurred she could never afterwards be quite sure, but she liked to believe and remember that *they,* the charming American boy and his pretty sister, had addressed her. The episode at any rate was epoch-making, and if she had actually encouraged them to speak to her, she never afterwards had occasion to regret it. One word rapidly led to another and when she had suggested with a daring reborn of this exciting contact that they visit a beer-garden together, the pair received the suggestion with the wildest enthusiasm. Over constantly refilled steins of delicious and frothy Pilsener, the young Americans and the Gräfin, her tiny feet in their laced boots swinging clear of the floor, had become the warmest of friends and soon she was questioning them eagerly in excellent English, become through disuse, a trifle rusty, in regard to the fabulous land of their birth, a land she had never visited even in its more conservative days.

America, it appeared from the account enthusiastically given to the Gräfin by her new friends, was kolossal in more ways than one. Other nations controlled the output of intoxicating liquors, deriving much revenue therefrom, and some nations, notably England, stipulated hours for drinking, but as drinking was prohibited in America, the government derived no benefit from the extraordinary amount of gins, wines, and whisky consumed and one could drink wherever and whatever and whenever one pleased.

The Gräfin received with delight this information

concerning a land which she had long entertained a desire
to visit and plied her young Americans with further inquiries to such purpose that presently she was acquainted
with the definitions of such words as bootlegger, speakeasy,
buffet-flat, racketeer, stinko, and ginny. The children's de-
scription of a typical cocktail party given by a débutante
friend pleased her so much that she listened with a certain
apathy to their further disclosures concerning tall towers,
stock exchanges where bull-fights were held, and the
machine-gun wars of the Chicago gangsters, but she woke
up with a start when they began to talk about Harlem.

The result of this encounter was a most terrific scene
with Fräulein Stupforsch and Maria who stood waiting for
her in front of the Grand Hotel Pupp when she walked a
little unsteadily up the gravel path. They bore her off in
disgrace to her apartment and lavished upon her their lustily audible disapproval of her conduct. It was at this very
moment that she conceived an unbreakable determination
to visit New York and without wasting time she commanded that cabins be booked on the boat which sailed
the soonest from the nearest port. Fräulein Stupforsch
threatened in vain to take her departure. The Gräfin refused to believe her. She resorted to tears. The Gräfin ignored them. Eventually, the companion appeared to be
won over and the Gräfin, satisfied with her temporary victory, retired and soon was dreaming that she was swimming around and around in a beer-vat. In the morn-

ing Fräulein Stupforsch renewed her opposition, rein-
forced with more subtle arguments, but without
avail. The Gräfin declined to retire from her position
and in the end she had her way, but she sailed without
Maria.

She kept to her bed during the sea-voyage. Never a
good traveller by water, this was the first time she had
undertaken so lengthy an excursion on the ocean, and she
did not enjoy herself. Nor were her first impressions of
America agreeable. As befitted one of her rank she was
entertained at once by members of the German-American
colony worthy of such an honour, but these excellent persons, many of them high-born, had not hitherto been acquainted with the Gräfin and they considerately tempered
their hospitality to suit an old lady. Dinners were announced and served at six o'clock and the elderly guest
whisked out of the house and back to her hotel by ten.
Moreover only the lightest food was provided. The menu
of a typical meal included the boiled breast of a chicken
with endive salad, a glass of Eltviller Langenstück Beeren
Auslese, and a sweet. After one of these repasts, the Gräfin
invariably returned to her hotel starving and was obliged to
eat another dinner at once. For the first time in her life she
began to long for filling German dishes: Fasanenpastete auf
Pumpernickel, Prager Schinken mit Kartoffelsalat, Bach-
forelle blau — zerlassene Butter, Thüringer Würstchen
— Orangen-Meerrettich, Schmorbraten mit Rotkraut,

✳ PARTIES ✳

Rebhühner mit Linsen, Sauerbraten mit Kartoffelklöss, Wiener Gugelhupf, Topfengalatschen, Zwetschgenknödel, Bayrische Dampfnudel, Schlagobers . . . The manners of these people were even more odious to the Gräfin than their dinners. Violently snobbish, they treated the Gräfin as if she were the present head of some provincial court to which they belonged. Time and again she came away from these houses in a rage which it was difficult for Fräulein Stupforsch to dispel, especially as the Fräulein found the Gräfin's rages incomprehensible, so nearly her descriptions of these dubious entertainments coincided with the Fräulein's own tastes.

As for bootleggers and speakeasies, Fräulein Stupforsch was adamant in her refusal to accompany her mistress on any tour of discovery in that dangerous direction. Such tentative inquiries in this regard as the Gräfin made among her German-American acquaintances were received with incredulity and amazement. It was as if, she realized quite early, they believed her to be mocking them. They could scarcely be expected to understand a distinguished old German lady's avowed interest in these degrading American institutions. As substitutes they suggested the Museum of Natural History, the Metropolitan Museum of Art, the Bronx Zoo, the Aquarium, and the concerts of the Philharmonic Society or the Philadelphia Symphony Orchestra, and were perhaps slightly offended when the Gräfin replied that animals, birds, and fish, alive or dead, no longer awakened her attention, except as food, that she felt no great desire ever to see another picture, and finally that she had no intention of wasting her declining years listening to Ravel's Bolero. The Gräfin might conceivably have demanded information concerning dives and resorts from the employees of her hotel, but she was convinced that this manœuvre would likewise prove futile. Apparently no one would believe that she actually meant what she said.

She was not, to be sure, compelled to do without liquor. Her new friends sent her bottles of Erdener Busslay 1921 and Piesporter Olk of the same excellent year and even a few French wines, Lanson 1920 and a not very good Pommard, but she was longing to drink gin in the festive surroundings described to her by the two young Americans she had met in Karlsbad. Unfortunately, she had not even learned the names of these Americans, let alone secured from them letters of introduction to their own special set.

So it was that on this particular evening, perhaps two weeks after her arrival in New York, the Gräfin felt inclined to kick this silly Fräulein Stupforsch while the latter was trying to draw on the noble boot to the end that dinner might be served, and she continued to scream, Nein, nein! and other expressions in excellent Hanoverian German and to wriggle her small feet in the literal face of the Fräulein's vehement and alarmed protestations. There is no knowing how long this state of affairs might have endured, had there not come an interruption in the form of a knock on the door.

Flushing from her exertion and her anxiety, Fräulein Stupforsch rose from her knees and crossed the room, accompanied by a continual beating on the door which had become a crescendo rhythmic tattooing. As soon as the Fräulein turned the knob, the door was violently flung open and the Gräfin became aware of the tempestuous entrance of a youth with a bundle. Slamming the door behind him, he stood with his back against it.

Fräulein Stupforsch emitted a slight scream.

Quit, can't you? the boy appealed to her. His face reflected the agony of a professional wrestler enduring the toe-grip.

The Gräfin spoke. What do you want, boy? she demanded.

They're after me, he exclaimed. They wants to take me for a ride.

Who's after you and why don't you want to go for a ride?

I dunno: bulls or hijackers, it's all the same. He frowned as he added, You wouldn't want to go for a ride neither.

So you're a bootlegger! the Gräfin cried in ecstasy, her smile bequeathing an amazing network of wrinkles to her face.

I works for one: the lad modified her assertion.

Well, I'd love to buy everything you've got, the Gräfin announced.

Might as well, the boy responded sullenly. I'd never get out alive to deliver it now.

What is it?

Fizz water.

What?

Champagne.

Will you stay to dinner?

The Gräfin offered this invitation with great dignity.

Might as well, the boy assented nervously. It's not so hot for me out in that hall, or in here either, if they saw me come in. If they get me they'll take me for a ride all right. . . . I killed a man last night, he added earnestly.

The Gräfin clapped her hands with delight. She was playing in great luck. She turned to address the bewildered and trembling Fräulein Stupforsch who had not yet moved from her position beside the door and who had not yet understood one word of what appeared to her to be a highly insane conversation.

Rufen Sie den Kellner, bitte.

This, at least, the Fräulein understood. Torrents of protestation poured from her lips.

The Gräfin reiterated more sternly: Rufen Sie den Kellner und schnüren Sie meine Stiefel.

As Fräulein Stupforsch, in tears, obeyed, the Gräfin beckoned the boy to approach and invited him to sit down near her. She became imbued at once, indeed, with great efficiency and vitality, commanding that the champagne be unwrapped and suggesting that at least three bottles be iced, and she ordered a dinner after her own liking, that is a dinner with a great deal of rich food. She even requested capriciously that a certain fan should be produced from one of her trunks.

In the meantime the bootlegger's apprentice sat silently curled up in an arm-chair. He was a pale, slender youth, with shiny, greased black hair, plastered flat over his head and cut in straight oily bangs low over his forehead. His black eyes were sunk deep in his head. His face was un-naturally white, save for the black circles around his eyes and his lips, the red of which, perhaps, was accentuated by his extreme pallor. The Gräfin noted more especially his remarkably graceful hands, with the abnormally long fingers tipped with pointed nails. He did not appear any longer to be in the least perturbed or surprised or pleased or astonished or annoyed or even curious.

Presently the waiters appeared with the table and the other appurtenances for dinner and this strange couple sat facing each other over the white cloth. They were sepa-rated, to be sure, by Fräulein Stupforsch, but she was quite unable to follow their conversation.

What is your name? the Gräfin demanded, helping her-self to stuffed celery.

Roy Fern, the boy replied.

How funny! she commented and then she explained, That's the name of my favourite perfume.

You wouldn't kid me, would you? he inquired, as he shoved a Cape Cod into his mouth with the aid of a butter-knife.

After the champagne was opened, he became more conversational and even volunteered a little autobiography.

As I was comin' up the freight-elevator, he said, the operator tipped me off to screw. So I get out at the wrong floor, chase myself down the hall, and hammer on your door. Say, I was lucky it was this one.

His face assumed an expression of perplexity.

I oughta call up Don, he explained.

Who's Don?

He's the swell egg I works for. He's reg'lar, he is.

The Gräfin was entranced. Figuratively, she thumbed her nose at Fräulein Stupforsch.

Oh, I want to meet him, she cried. We'll drive over there right after dinner.

❊ *THREE* ❊

Donald Bliss was known as the handsomest bootlegger in New York, but the ladies who were clever enough to remember the old proverb, Handsome is as handsome does, had no cause to complain in the end. He was the son of a retired police officer who had consecrated his offspring at an early age either to politics or the priesthood. Donald began his apprenticeship for his alternative careers by emptying waste-paper-baskets, running errands, and pasting stamps on envelopes for a Tammany Boss. A little later — in his eighteenth year, to be exact — the boy's interest in the daughter of a neighbour's family led to more or less serious complications. The parents of this female were sturdy German folk who would have preferred to see their child married in honest wedlock, but Donald's father, not without difficulty, although he was well versed in the practices of the third degree, succeeded in persuading them that such a step, in view of the highly inflammable and irresponsible nature of his son, would be extremely injudicious and bound to lead to disaster. In due time, therefore — not, to be sure, before Donald had become a father and was tired of her — the girl was immured in a convent where, under the name of Sister Mary Magdalen Donalda, she engaged in many good works and devout devices.

✳ *PARTIES* ✳

In some way or other an inkling of this history reached the ears of the mighty fellow of Tammany by whom Donald was employed and, admiring the talent for intrigue displayed therein, he sent for the boy who, ushered into the presence, confirmed the excellent impression his deeds had already made, by blushing. The Boss deftly inquired into the young man's ambitions and discovered, not entirely to his astonishment, that they were entirely sympathetic to the expressed ideals of Tammany. Thereafter Donald was assigned to places nearer the throne, carrying verbal messages, of a character too special to be entrusted to writing, from one wigwam to another, listening in occasionally to extraordinary secrets, bearing the burden of remembering verbatim lengthy telephonic communications, being admitted, indeed, to the company of that slowly growing group of youths destined one day to penetrate the City Hall or the Capitol at Albany or the White House, or even better yet to become a distinguished racketeer. There can be but little doubt that at least one of these intentions would have been realized eventually, had not the Boss's daughter acquired a serious attachment for the police officer's handsome son. Moreover, there probably would have been no serious objection on any hand to the publishing of the banns, if an unfortunate obstacle had not intervened in the shape of the Boss's daughter's husband, himself a seneschal of Tammany and by no means ignorant of the pleasant relationship existing between his wife and

Donald. In view of his natural feelings in the matter and the fact that his knowledge of the circumstances made it difficult to overlook them, it was thought to be the part of wisdom for Donald to retire from active politics, for the time being, to devote his very considerable talents to a career in which his appetite for women would not be disturbing. So it was that, with backing and approval from the very highest sources, Donald became a bootlegger.

His success in this field was immediate, especially in families where the women of the household occupied the position of wine steward, but men also liked Donald, more particularly men without wives or sweethearts or sisters, or men who did not care for women at all. So Donald soon built up a very pretty trade, but what with his extravagances and the sums he was forced to pay to those higher up for tribute he did not at once acquire riches.

His modest place of business, known as the Wishbone, occupying the third floor of a brown-stone house in the East Fifties, was similar to those maintained by many of his confrères. To be more concrete, the place was furnished with a sufficient number of chairs and tables of Grand Rapids manufacture, a piano, a radio, a phonograph, a few cheap rugs, and some framed lithographs of nude women. The seven rooms of the apartment were arranged on a corridor so that it was possible, when desirable, to keep the customers more or less apart. Usually, however, the guests were pleased to mingle in the big front room. Many of them, indeed, were well acquainted with each other. They were served, from a pantry in the back, by boys who had no immediate means of support and who turned, not unrewarded, to Donald for assistance. He put them to work passing drinks, washing glasses, or delivering packages of liquor, modern Ganymedes that they were, to one Jove after another. Sometimes this led to something.

The clientele of the Wishbone might be described as cosmopolitan. Perhaps bohemian — if one may revive a worn out epithet that once meant a great deal — would be a more exact word. There gathered not only many of the very best people — whose names appeared on the passenger lists of the Majestic or the Ile de France and who headed the reports of balls at Palm Beach or those of Reno divorces — but also others far richer, but not so well known to a tabloid public, and yet others: painters, writers, chauffeurs, actors, sailors, soldiers, and firemen. Neither Donald nor his customers suffered from race prejudice. The group was held together — and this is probably true of all successful salons — by the personality of the host. Donald did not flatter his clients. Rather he controlled them with a kind of good-natured banter, always a trifle disturbing to self-esteem, occasionally downright insolent.

On the same evening that Roy Fern had so unceremoniously joined the Gräfin von Pulmernl und Stilzernl for dinner, a representative gathering occupied Donald's large front room. There was Simone Fly, a slim creature in

silver sequins from which protruded, at one end, turquoise blue legs and, from the other, extremely slender
arms and a chalk-white (almost green) face, with a de-
praved and formless mouth, intelligent eyes, and a rage
of cropped red hair. Simone Fly resembled a gay Death.
There was King Swan, the chauffeur, one of Donald's
pals, an honest fellow built for business (when it came to
the cauliflower industry) on the whole kindly and not in-
tentionally humorous. King was thirty-five, had blue eyes,
pink cheeks, and yellow hair. Of his habit of stowing
cigarette ashes neatly in the cuffs of his trousers, a certain
wag remarked that this was Swan's way. In one corner of
the room at a table under a calendar which advertised the
Equitable Life Insurance Company sat a lugubrious soldier in khaki, muttering to himself from time to time
something about early mass and Governor's Island, the
while he consumed bar-glasses filled to the brim with what
is known as neat whisky. Talking to Simone was a young
man whom nobody knew very much about except that he
played the piano well. He was affectionately dubbed
Beauty Butcher, apparently because his name was Marma-
duke and he was very ugly. He differed from most other
mortals in boasting two sets of teeth, one of which had
grown inside the other. Donald, as usual, drifted in and
out of the room.

Simone sprawled on a wooden chair, her turquoise legs
stuck out in front of her, her head waving from side to

side, rooster fashion, while she flourished a highball in her right hand.

Stop that damned radio! she shrieked. I'm sick of hearing the Mosquito Paraders.

Hey, bring me another rickey, Freddie. King Swan hailed a boy with bright red hair parted in the centre.

I hope you're through driving customers tonight, suggested Donald. They'll certainly get a good ride with a souse like you.

Six o'clock mass, ten o'clock mass, twelve o'clock mass, droned the soldier. I looked at the clock and the clock struck . . .

Oh, shut up! Simone cried. Turn off that radio, Don. Did you hear about Rosalie Keith? she unexpectedly demanded of Beauty Butcher who shared her table, at the same time dropping her highball glass to the floor where it crashed.

No. What about her?

Freddie wiped up the floor and presently brought her a fresh whisky and soda. It was such a commonplace for Simone to break glasses or to spill drinks that one seldom remarked when she did so.

What about who?

You said Rosalie Keith . . . prompted Beauty Butcher.

Oh, yes. . . . You must quit kissing parrots, Beauty.

I never did.

More likely poufs.

I never did.

Well, anyway Rosalie asks David to dinner every night. Hopes to make him. Rilda comes too, without being invited.

He brings her?

Hell, no. She brings another man. Rosalie's frightfully sore, but what can she do?

Let's all go to Harlem, suggested King Swan.

Not me, said Beauty Butcher. I like mammy songs, but I don't care for mammy palaver.

To hell with what you like, cried Simone, running her long white hands blazing with great red and blue stones through her tousled hair, and dropping another glass in the process. I'll go with you, King.

Say, you must be nuts, you kids, Donald paused in the doorway long enough to remark. Harlem at eight P.M.! That's like Hollywood in 1840.

Aw, shut up, Don, Simone screamed, and turn off that damn radio.

All right, *all* right, Donald responded. Then, to Freddie, You're permanently engaged as floor-wiper for Madame Fly, pl-lease.

Don's too fresh, too goddam fresh, commented Simone.

He's right about Harlem anyway, said Beauty Butcher. This is a helluvan hour to go to Harlem.

I don't know whether he is or not, Simone argued

obstinately. It's early, but the early bird catches the worm.

The son also rises, Donald sapiently observed.

Six o'clock mass, seven o'clock mass, and then Governor's Island for me, droned the soldier.

Aw, shut up, and turn off that radio, shrieked Simone. Let's put Ethel Waters on the phonograph. Am I Blue?

I dunno, said King Swan. There's a girl up there now you oughta hear. She does her hair so her head looks like a wet seal and when she pounds the piano the dawn comes up like thunder. Say, she rocks the box, and tosses it, you can bet, and jumps it through hoops, and wait till you hear her sing Subway Papa and then go back to the farm and tell the folks and your pappy'll hitch lions to the plough instead o' mules.

Well, King, you certainly are full of poetic thoughts tonight, Simone commented, and if it ever gets late enough and I can get drunk I'll go to Harlem with you to listen to the wet seal.

Y'oughta hear her yodel. God, she gurgles and coughs an ya-up-i-diddies till you feel ready to push any good enterprise along and Clarv Chenavent barks and does his back head-kick.

Well, King, I'll go with you, if it ever gets late enough, Simone reiterated.

Suddenly the soldier stood up somewhat unsteadily and looked about him with great energy.

Say, where's the toilet? he demanded in a loud voice.

Go down the hall, Freddie advised him, till you see a door with a sign where it says: Beggars and Pedlars not admitted. That's it.

Speakin' of toilets, King Swan went on, flicking his ashes carefully into his trousers cuff, and sipping his rickey, I was in the toilet at Connie's last night and . . .

Say, this is gettin' intimate, Donald remarked. What were you doin' in a toilet? You'd think this place was Some Limericks or Lady Chatterley's Lover.

Shut up, Don, cried Simone. Quit ridin' King.

the boy was deliverin' a reg'lar monologue while he brushed the customers and passed the soap and combs and towels. It was so swell I had to stop to listen and everybody handed the kid fifty instead of a quarter. One man give 'im a dollar. Well, later I went back and there he was. The same line. Reg'lar vodeville. Smokey wise-cracks, if you get me.

The soldier staggered back to his place in the corner under the calendar.

Well, I asked him: How come? And he informs me.

Gee, sneers Donald from the doorway, aping Jimmie Durante, some in-former.

He informs me, King sternly persisted, that he'd got a reg'lar playwriter to put it down for him and he had learned it, and he pays the playwriter two dollars a month for the privilege of usin' the act.

I gotta hear it, cried Simone in rapture.

It's the gents' toilet, Donald reminded her.

Stop kissing parrots, Simone came back with, and shut off that . . .

Donald expectedly obeyed her.

There's a sign in a bird-store window down the street, King remarked, which reads: No more parrots. Come in and have a good time with the pets.

I'm going to get that to paste on Rosalie's door, Simone promised, in ecstasy.

Six o'clock mass, groaned the soldier, and his head fell forward on his arm laid across the table.

Here tis, announced Simone.

Damfitaint, retorted Beauty.

At this juncture the bell rang and presently red-haired Freddie could be heard adjusting the chains and various locks on the door. The entrance of David and Hamish was somewhat spectacular.

Donald, cried David, where's the kid's body?

Donald blinked and regarded the newcomers with amazement.

I certainly thought I was never goin' to see you again, David, he said.

Hamish was searching the room and the corridor behind him with his eyes.

Nonsense, Donald, David expostulated. I mean Fern. Where is he?

Fern's all right. Somebody telephoned this morning to say you were killed.

Somebody telephoned me this morning that Fern was killed, Hamish replied indignantly, some one who said he was Donald Bliss. It sounded like you too, he went on hotly.

Well, it wasn't, the bootlegger retorted doggedly. I don't know what to make of this. Fern ain't here now, but he's alive all right.

Aw, go jump out a window! cried Simone.

Why, hello, Simone, you old pepper-pot, David called out. I didn't see you. Then again to Donald: *Something* happened in Harlem last night, he explained. Somebody's dead all right. Was Roy there?

He *thinks* he was, Donald responded, drawing his forefinger significantly under his nose, but I know damned well he wasn't. He was here all night.

But I saw him, David insisted.

Oh, come now, Hamish expostulated, you were blind. You couldn't see anything.

Well, perhaps a little, David admitted, but I'll swear I saw Roy.

He swears he saw you, retorted Donald. He even says he killed you. I let him get away with the idea, but you don't suppose I'd let him out tonight if I wasn't sure, do you?

Say, Freddie, gimme 'nuther drink, cried Simone who

had now assumed an incredibly startling attitude, with one leg over the back of the chair, her head resting on the arm, her drooping wrist jingling with silver and glass bracelets. Her upturned face in the amber light of the speakeasy parlor had now become absolutely green. Beauty Butcher had taken his departure.

There's something funny about all this, Hamish announced, as he attacked a glass of Pernod and water. By God, I'm going to look into this. There's been dirty work somewhere.

Sure there has, Donald agreed serenely. There's always dirty work. After awhile we'll all go lookin' up the corpse, so David can confess and crash the electric chair.

David grinned broadly, his fingers closing automatically on a glass which Freddie had placed in his hand. Slumping into a seat, he said, I hate to think of some guy getting bumped off and nobody knows who or where or how or not even exactly when. It oughta get in the papers or something. Where's Roy? Perhaps he knows more than he told you.

He oughta been back hours ago. He only went around the corner to deliver some champagne. I called up the party — Senator Humperdinck — but he ain't seen him at all.

Donald reflectively lighted a big black cigar.

Maybe he's pinched, suggested King Swan who had followed the conversation with interest.

That's a cheerful thought, and maybe I didn't forget it, Donald admitted.

At this juncture the telephone bell rang. Freddie left the room to answer it, and returned to report that Roy was arriving presently with some German nobility.

Was he tight? Donald demanded.

I'll say he was, Freddie reported. Stinkin'.

Another case of fizz gone to hell, growled Donald. I'll break his goddam neck. Him and his German queens!

I wish to God, groaned David, you hadn't told me he was coming back here with these Germans. It's going to be rich and I hate to miss it. I gotta lot to do. I gotta dine with Rosalie . . .

You dined there last night, corrected Hamish.

and my wife killed herself this morning and I s'pose I oughta look up a coupla morticians.

She *said* she killed herself, Hamish corrected him.

Rilda's such a liar, put in Simone Fly unexpectedly.

You shut up, cried David in a fury. You keep out of this.

Aw, shut up yourself. Blaaa! Simone looked extraordinarily happy.

Bite him in the ankle, advised Donald.

Simone revised her attitude, so that she could sit up and scowl, dropping another glass in the process.

I really oughta do something about something, muttered David.

Well, said Donald, smiling broadly, if you're too busy to meet the Berlin queens, I guess I can receive 'em alone.

Hear! Hear! cried the chauffeur. Donald Bliss, assisted by King Swan, receives party of German queens in his palatial speakeasy. A good time was had.

Say, don't get snooty on me, Donald, protested David. That damned bitch, Rosalie Keith, and my beloved wife can wait.

The outer doorbell rang.

Enter royalty preceded by slaves on elephants and camels! Hamish announced.

But it was Rilda.

David whistled as he placed his glass carefully on a table. Then he rose.

Hello, Rilda . . . and his voice was sympathetic as he added, I kiss your hand, madame.

There's music to that, Hamish, also risen, explained.

I know, said David impatiently.

Rilda was as taut as Con Colleano about to cross the high wire, as prepared for tragedy as Rachel entering the theatre to play Phèdre.

A lot you care whether I die or not, was her greeting.

Listen, my pretty, David said, I was just telling the crowd that if it weren't for the imminent approach of the German nobility I was going to hunt you out.

About time, too, David. . . Rilda's voice was

tremulous. . . It doesn't seem as if I'd seen you alone in years. We meet at parties and speakeasies. We love and eat and live at parties. Probably we'll die at a party too. . . She spoke bitterly.

Now, my angel, let's keep this a little light opera.

It's quite light opera enough for me, cried Rilda fiercely. A fine mess you were when you left Rosalie's last night.

Were you there? David demanded in astonishment, adding, You couldn't have been asked.

I was there all right. I went to Harlem with you. I was the girl in pink.

Then . . ? His face published his pleasure.

I dropped you off at the Plum Pudding to meet Hamish.

You see, remarked Hamish blandly, as if it had always been his idea, you didn't kill anybody after all.

Will you two ever stop ironing your dirty clothes in public and let Don put Ethel Waters on the phonograph? demanded Simone, flinging her arms about like semaphores out of order, and kicking her shoes off.

Donald gave her a withering look and suggested to Freddie that he bring her another drink. She'll pass out soon, he said to the group. If she don't, we'll chloroform her.

The soldier under the calendar woke up, supported his chin on his palm, and yelled loudly for more whisky.

I gotta get to seven o'clock mass, he said. Father . . .
The remaining words were a meaningless mumble.

I thought it was tonight, David remarked. I was going
to Rosalie's.

It might as well have been, my only husband, Rilda replied. David had long since slumped back into his chair.
She seated herself, removed her gloves, and began to
drink the highball that Freddie had prepared for her.
You poured enough champagne on the Aubusson, she
continued.

Champagne's good for tapestry.

I remember you slapped Mrs. Pollanger on her lovely
old back, Hamish put in.

David roared. Not Isabel!

Isabel, Rilda insisted. She was smiling now. You called
the butler by his first name . . .

How did I ever know it?

You didn't. You called him Reginald. The joke of it is
that his name is Percival.

Rilda, my pet white doe, you're as sweet as springtime
in Buda-Pesth. You have such a satisfying sense of humour.
How did I get out of Rosalie's?

You said you had to meet Roy Fern and take him to
Paris. You dashed away without your overcoat and I followed you. By the way, David, he's dead.

You'll see how dead he is, said Donald. He'll be here
any minute. He thinks he killed David, he added.

It's all very strange, Rilda remarked. She regarded Donald with greater interest.

How did you get home? David demanded. I remember the girl in pink was blotto.

Well, I was in a taxi and anyway I could walk and think and remember, Rilda responded.

I'll bet Rosalie was drunk too, chuckled David.

Oh, Rosalie! was Rilda's contemptuous retort.

Who isn't drunk these days? Hamish demanded rhetorically.

I'm not, shrieked Simone. Let's go to Harlem.

Much too early, King Swan assured her.

The doorbell sounded.

Here's your elephants and camels, suggested Donald.

It proved to be. This time the customers were rewarded with a somewhat blurred vision of German nobility. The Gräfin entered on the fragile arm of Roy Fern. She wore a little black bonnet crowned with a wreath of pink roses over her waved and hennaed hair and a cape of beaver over her black taffeta dress. Her smiling face, less than five feet from the floor, was screwed into a smiling network of wrinkles.

Turning to David in great joy, Roy cried, You're alive! I didn't kill you!

David smiled. Not yet, my boy.

I'm glad, David, the boy assured him.

Well, you oughta be with that snow storm you got raging around inside of you, growled Donald. What'd you do with the case of champagne you were delivering to the Senator?

Don't scold him. . . The Gräfin protectively placed her arm around Roy's shoulder. . . I won't have it. I bought the champagne. I've paid for it. . . She waved a cheque in the air.

Donald, dazed, accepted the currency.

This scene is peculiarly picturesque, David drawled, but what does it mean?

I . . . Roy began.

Now you keep still, Donald urged him, until we're alone, if we ever are.

The group stared in amazement at the Gräfin as, seemingly perfectly at home, she sat down, untied her bonnet, flung it on the table, and demanded a drink. As usual her feet swung clear of the floor.

I knew it, she cried, looking about her. This is the place I dreamed of. Oh, you dear boy, come here.

An embarrassed Roy Fern awkwardly approached the throne. When he was within reach, she clutched his arms, drew him towards her and kissed his cheek. Released, he blushed furiously, rubbed his face with his hands, and fled to a corner where he stood trembling.

Which of you is the actual bootlegger? demanded the Gräfin.

Donald bowed from the waist down. He had not

attended moving picture exhibitions without learning something.

Would you like some Rhine wine, madame? he inquired politely.

It doesn't matter. Anything will be quite all right now. Anything. So this is really a speakeasy. . . Tears started to the old lady's eyes. . . I am so happy, she explained, wiping her eyes with her lace handkerchief. I haven't been so happy since the Count died. I mean . . . Well, you know what I mean. And now that I'm here and have met all Roy's nice friends I hope we can go right on knowing each other and staying up nights and drinking together.

To the health of the Countess, cried David, rising.

To the health of the Uh-ha, the others cried more or less in unison.

They all lifted their glasses and drank the proposed health.

Where did you meet the lady, Roy? David demanded.

I run into her, Roy explained truthfully. I just run into her. I'm awful glad it wasn't *you* I killed, David, awful glad.

Aw, shut up, cried Simone, staggering over to the table of the military man. I'm going out with the unknown soldier. Blaaaa!

You didn't kill anybody, David assured Roy, not a soul. I killed. I am the murderer.

David, you damned idiot . . . Rilda began, but she was interrupted.

The Gräfin burst into peals of hysterical laughter, shrill and without resonance, like the Bell Song from Lakmé rendered by a coloratura soprano in her decline. Tapping David lightly on the shoulder with her fan, she let him know that she understood the rules of this new game.

It was I who killed him, she cried. Ja, it was I. I killed him.

Jeese! moaned Roy, O Jeese!

Give the little murderess a hand! suggested Donald.

✳ *FOUR* ✳

The first cocktail party given by the Gräfin in her hotel-apartment impressed those who attended it in various ways. It cannot be denied that it was one of the most unusual affairs of this short and tempestuous New York winter. Even the unexpected presence of Fräulein Stupforsch did not serve to embarrass the guests. It is even possible that most of them were unaware of this phenomenon. An added, if somewhat impermanent, air of respectability was given to the occasion by the appearance of a number of the Gräfin's German-American acquaintances. Her hesitation about inviting them had been transient. After all, she was too hospitable not to wish to show her appreciation to a few of her dinner hostesses and their families, whose intentions towards her, however unsatisfactory the execution, had always been kindly. It is not unlikely that these German-Americans enjoyed themselves thoroughly, whatever they may have said later by way of derogation.

Fräulein Stupforsch, waiting up two nights earlier, had been appalled, by the return at an unseemly hour of the Gräfin, indubitably somewhat under the influence of intoxicating liquor. Her feelings proved to be incommunicable. She had wept her protests into unheeding ears. The Gräfin had enjoyed herself far too much to suffer from vain regrets. The next morning, when the Gräfin began to employ the telephone in behalf of her projected cocktail party, was even more unendurable for Fräulein Stupforsch, but neither her companion's tearful entreaties nor the fact that she herself was undergoing digestive pains as a result of her recent dissipation served to chill the ardour of the Gräfin's enthusiasm. It is likely that Fräulein Stupforsch would have perished from a heart attack had she understood the significance of that phrase so often repeated: Bring anybody you like.

I shall feel quite all right day after tomorrow, the Gräfin condescended to explain to her companion, and I have promised my friends I shall give them a party. The Gräfin von Pulmernl und Stilzernl always keeps her word.

A little after twelve o'clock on the day set for the event, the red-haired Freddie and Roy Fern began to make a series of appearances accompanied by divers and sundry cases of liquor of various varieties that had been recommended by Donald. By three o'clock the apartment was provided with all the essential ingredients for an orgy of the first class.

Donald, as bidden, himself arrived early and at once set to work to concoct some most ingenious mixtures.

I know nothing about cocktails, the Gräfin had explained to him. Fräulein Stupforsch has never heard of a cocktail. You must mix them.

Donald had been more than willing, and on the day in

question, after a wondering glance or two at Fräulein Stupforsch — he had never seen anybody in the least like her
— he went to work.

You're going to have a lot of people here today who
don't know each other, ain't you? he demanded.

The Gräfin assented.

Well, then, he suggested, we'd better make 'em plenty
strong in the beginning. Later it won't matter.

So he poured gin, bitters, absinthe, Italian and French
vermouth, Scotch, rye, Bourbon, bacardi, and Swedish
punch, fairly indiscriminately into huge punch-bowls already containing orange- and lemon- and grapefruit juice
and would presently contain great chunks of ice. These
bowls reposed on a long, white-clothed table, on which
provision was made, in the way of ingredients and glasses,
for those who preferred highballs to cocktails. There were
also trays of canapés, sandwiches, and other appetizers.
With two waiters under him, Donald was put in charge of
this auspicious outlay. The Gräfin had also compromised
sufficiently with Fräulein Stupforsch's prejudices to permit
her to preside over a table where coffee, tea, chocolate, and
petits fours were dispensed. It must be admitted that poor
Fräulein Stupforsch had very little to do.

When everything was ready, as the clock on the marble
mantelpiece was striking five, the Gräfin stood in the centre of the red carpet ready to receive. Wearing a mauve tea-
gown with floating ribbon-ends and bows, clusters of violets

here and there, and a lace train, with her corseted figure, high, laced boots, and the wreath of tiny, pink roses in her hennaed hair, she resembled, to those who could remember that far back — and a few who could were present — no one quite so much as Mrs. General Tom Thumb, unless it might have been Mrs. Frank Leslie reciting Mrs. Wilcox's The Birth of the Opal.

The first arrivals were Mr. and Mrs. Friedrich Oberhalter and their pretty daughter Irma, with her flaxen hair and pale blue eyes. After greeting their hostess, they were presented to Donald who suggested a cocktail.

Friedrich Oberhalter, who had an eye and a moustache like those of the late Kaiser, accepted with alacrity. The ladies exhibited a wistful diffidence, but when urged by Donald, they no longer refused.

What do you think of Mengelberg's Brahms? Mrs. Oberhalter demanded of Donald.

As he handed her a cocktail which contained among other ingredients absinthe, rye whisky, gin, and Italian vermouth, he replied with a broad wink, I wouldn't dare tell you.

Mrs. Stumpelmayer was now steam-rolling her ponderous way across the floor, holding her great bosom well in advance and waving a handkerchief fragrant with Floris's Bean Blossom, as she greeted the Gräfin.

My dear, she exclaimed in her soft Bavarian

49

German, how delightful to find you so well! And cocktails! she added, with every evidence of surprise and delight.

The Gräfin was not averse to compliments, whatever the source. Her smile caused the habitual network of wrinkles to map her face, as she replied: Why not, my dear? Man lebt nur einmal.

Oh, how witty, Gräfin, and what beautiful chrysanthemums! Mrs. Stumpelmayer cried, staring very hard at Donald Bliss.

Approaching him, she said, How very extraordinary that any one so good looking as you are should be unknown to me.

Now, you know, you caught me thinking the same thing, retorted Donald. Have a drink. It's good for your figure.

She accepted the glass.

Ha! Ha! laughed Friedrich Oberhalter, stroking his moustache violently, gallantry is coming to the New World after all.

Mrs. Stumpelmayer took in the fact of her friend's immediate presence with immense displeasure.

Friedrich, she responded haughtily, I didn't see you.

Nor us, perhaps? Mrs. Oberhalter inquired.

Really . . . Mrs. Stumpelmayer was in dismay.

Oh, Olga! the ladies cried and pounced upon her.

In the meantime a stream of people was swiftly filling

up the lake of the room, and the Gräfin, tired of hand-shaking, had about reached the point where she had deter-mined to sit down and enjoy herself, when there occurred a transposition of key in the party which completely changed its mood. Rilda arrived, very gay in a tight-fitting grey velvet dress with a broad band of silver fox around the hem and a grey velvet hat sheathing her green-yellow hair and her grey-green eyes, on the arms of Hamish and David. All three were sufficiently intoxicated to be entirely careless of appearances.

Adele, my dear! Rilda flung out affectionate arms and embraced the quite willing Gräfin. Then: Where did you find those chrysanthemums? They're as big as cabbages and as shaggy as sheep-dogs and as brightly coloured as . . . as . . .

As diphtheria, suggested Hamish tentatively.

As dolphins in the Gulf Stream, was Rilda's final choice of simile.

Anyway, Adele, I've never before seen so many Cen-tral Europeans, announced David. You should have en-gaged a band to play Heilige Nacht out of tune. It looks like a German prison camp.

They wouldn't be Germans in a German prison camp, argued Hamish.

What would they be?

Oh, Russians or English or . . .

Nonsense, cried David with great finality. Of course

they would be Germans in a German prison camp. Why else . . ?

The Gräfin tapped him playfully on the shoulder with her fan, and he quite forgot what he had intended to say.

Rilda had already wandered to the further side of the room.

My dear children, will you have a drink? the Gräfin inquired.

As she escorted them to the table, David squeezed her hand and said, Dear Adele, Queen of the Murder Ring, I *am* glad to see you. . . He struck an attitude. . . Then to Donald: Where's Roy?

I should know where that one is, Donald shouted to make himself heard over the din of conversation. I think he plans to marry into the German nobility.

A tall gentleman with sideburns, who resembled not a little certain famous portraits of the Emperor Maximilian, started perceptibly when he thought he heard this remark.

I beg your pardon? He cupped his ear and leaned closer to Donald.

I beg yours, Donald replied. It was my fault.

You ups to him, suggested David.

But, the gentleman expostulated, I only . . .

No buts about it, Donald said bluntly. I tell you it was my fault.

Nobody is to blame, shouted the gentleman pleasantly,

for something that cannot be said to have occurred. I only wanted to make sure that I heard you aright just now. Would you repeat the statement, sir, if you please?

Oh, that! David responded for him, while Donald was dextrously shaking a special cocktail. He was speaking, David explained, of the Swedish Crown Prince, Fougère Royale, who is expected at any minute now.

I wasn't aware, muttered the whiskered gentleman, obviously quite stunned by this information, that the Gräfin had actually invited us to meet royalty. Crossing the room, he repeated the report as he moved, and lips, expressing astonishment, could be seen on every hand forming the words, The Swedish Crown Prince. David himself had already begun to believe it.

Is it true? Irma Oberhalter was inquiring of Donald, with a very tender look in her pale blue eyes.

What? Donald demanded, his eyes on the shaker he was manipulating.

About the Swed —

Something about the quality of the voice impelled Donald to look up now, and he replied: Sure, if you want to believe it. . . A further inspection of the expression in the pale blue eyes led him to add, How do you like the Casino in the Park?

It depends.

I mean with me.

I'd go almost anywhere you asked me to, Mr. Bliss,

except to the theatre. She laughed, as she continued, I hate to hold hands in the theatre, don't you? Donald, we've got so little time. Please give me another cocktail.

Donald laughed. Why, kid, you can drink all night if you want to. There's plenty of time and plenty of hooch. I oughta know. I made it.

Donald, she inquired, will you marry me?

What a bright kid! Where did you get that line? . . . He looked at her with admiration. . . How do you know I'm not married already?

In the meantime Rilda stood in a window by the side of a tall, handsome German lad who only needed silver armour to resemble Lohengrin or a lieutenant's uniform to look like something romantic from a play.

My husband is such a rotter, Rilda remarked, as she drained her tenth cocktail. He's always drunk. Why, the other night he killed a man.

The tall German seemed bewildered and perhaps a little alarmed.

In a duel, perhaps?

In a duel! Rilda's tone was one of ironic disgust. Don't make me queasy. He was just drunk in Harlem.

Oh, a Nigger. . . The German was obviously relieved. . . You are unhappily married then, Mrs. . . ? he inquired.

Westlake. I should say I am. Call me Rilda.

The young man adjusted a monocle and gazed at her.

I'd be delighted, Rilda, he said. When will you take tea with me?

Oh, don't mention tea, Rilda exclaimed petulantly. I don't drink tea or smoke opium. Never!

I mean in my apartment. George Bellows lithographs. A phonograph playing the Caprice Viennois. A warm fire. Tea for two. Orchids. A bear-skin rug. A glass of sherry. . . . He recited these items very much in the manner of a dramatic reader attacking Baudelaire's Le Balcon.

You darling Central European! cried Rilda. I believe you are trying to seduce me romantically. Nobody has ever done it before. I must thank Adele for this delicious experience.

Then you'll come? He was standing back of the tea-table and stretching his arm past Fräulein Stupforsch, he extracted several lumps of sugar from the sugar-bowl. One of these he put in his mouth and crunched. The remainder he put in his pocket.

Of course, I'll come, Rilda responded, regarding this performance with curiosity. I won't promise to be seduced, but I'll be delighted to let you have a try at it.

Is your husband here today? he inquired.

Certainly, she replied stiffly. I came with him. He's drunk. He's always drunk. . . She appeared to be reflecting. . . So am I, most of the time, she added.

At this moment there was another diversion in the room. It was perfectly apparent, by the behaviour of the crowd, that there had been an important arrival, and Rilda turned to see Simone Fly, in a brilliant red frock and béret, her face paler than ever, her mouth more formless, enter with Midnight Blue, the moving picture star.

Midnight Blue was everything, except perhaps sober, that the public could demand of one of its favourite cinema actresses. She was beautiful and daring and smartly dressed and even amusing. At the moment she was swathed in velvet of the colour that her name suggested and carried an ebony cane with a diamond-studded tip. She and Simone leaned rather heavily against each other as they made unsteady but triumphant progress across the floor.

I want you to meet the Countess, Simone assured her friend. Blaa!

What does that mean — Blaaa? demanded Midnight Blue.

Blaa, that means blaa. Blaaaa! I want you to meet the Countess. Simone shook her head ominously.

The Gräfin gratified this ambition by joining them.

Midnight Blue, sweetest little girl in Hollywood, meet the great Countess of . . . well, you know . . . Simone flung her arms about wildly, pirouetted on one toe, and reiterated, Blaaa!   Blaaa!

What is the latest Hollywood diversion? inquired David who was standing behind the Gräfin.

Let me see . . . the star appeared to ponder. . . I think it would be the toilet-paper races. You select two

sides with captains and provide each person with a roll of
swell toilet-paper and then there is a referee with a stop-
watch to see which side can unroll the most within a given
time. It's a practical game, she added wistfully and, without being asked, smiled prettily, removed her hat, sat down
to the piano, opened it, ran her hands artlessly a few times
over the keys, and sang a few notes very loudly of something that sounded like Vissi d'Arte, before she was joined
on the piano bench by Friedrich Oberhalter.

Another buzz of whispering around the room announced the arrival of the Crown Prince of Sweden.

Roy Fern, extremely pale and fragile-appearing, his long
white fingers clutching convulsively at his thighs, came in
very quietly and stared about him in amazement at the
sensation his entrance had created, for the crowd fell back
opening a path, certain individuals whom he had never
seen before were actually bowing low to him, and Mrs.
Stumpelmayer attempted as much of a curtsy as her
rheumatic limbs would permit her to execute.

What is it? What is it? Roy demanded anxiously of
David.

They're glad to see you, David explained. Then, holding high his glass, he proposed to the crowd, Das Farn-
kraut!

The other guests echoed, Prosit! as they lifted their
cocktail glasses and drained them in unison. In an effort to
replenish the diminished supply, Donald and the two

waiters worked valiantly at pouring the contents of inter-esting-looking bottles into the punch-bowls.

The Gräfin was utterly delighted with her party by now, and she took pleasure in presenting Roy to her friends who surrounded him. Roy, with a highball glass full of cocktails in his hand, asked no more questions.

Rilda had discovered that her German was named Sieg-fried, Siegfried Gerhardt.

He was curious about Roy Fern.

Everybody wants to know about him, Rilda responded. My husband invited him to go abroad and then killed him.

The fine, expansive, resonant voice of David Westlake could now be heard booming, although he was talking into Hamish's ear: I tell you Rosalie is a slut, a fat slut. I wish to God I'd never seen her face.

What did I tell you? Rilda demanded triumphantly of Siegfried. Is he or isn't he?

She hurled her glass across the room. Aimed at David, it struck the distinguished gentleman with whiskers who gave Rilda a reproachful glance before he collapsed on the floor.

Can't you be careful? Donald inquired of Rilda. Even the rich have feelings.

He may have hæmophilia for all she knows, suggested David.

Aided by the two waiters, Donald succeeded in carrying the gentleman into the bedroom where he lay on the bed and sobbed.

The rotter! I'll go away with you tonight, Rilda assured Siegfried.

Not tonight, the German corrected her. Tomorrow at tea-time. A bear-skin rug. The Caprice Viennois. Orchids. A glass of sherry.

Oh, to hell with it! cried Rilda. Tonight without the trimmings.

But I don't want you tonight, Siegfried argued plaintively. I simply can't have you tonight. I've made other plans for tonight.

Change them. I swear to God I'll go tonight, Rilda cried.

Go where? Hamish inquired over her shoulder.

I'm leaving David for ever, she cried hysterically. I can't put up with it any longer, all this . . . she swept her arm around in a vague gesture . . . publicity, notoriety. I'm going to Rumania with Siegfried.

But, protested the German, I'm not going to Rumania. I have an engagement with Aunt Caroline.

What the hell do I care about your Aunt Caroline? She can go with us if she likes.

What about David? Hamish demanded bitterly.

I don't know, was Rilda's careless response. I suppose he's going to Harlem to kill Roy Fern. He usually does at this hour.

At the piano, Simone, a cross between a poster by

Chéret and a caricature by Toulouse-Lautrec — in a successful attempt to better the expression, She has chien, Claire Madrilena had once said of Simone, She has all the dogs! — was waving an empty glass around the halo of her pink hair and shrieking: Take Lindbergh! Take gorgonzola! Take Jimmie Walker! Take platinum! Take Chirico! Take the Fratellini! Take . . .

Midnight Blue struck a chord, removed the man's arm that encircled her waist, and suggested, Take novocaine!

Take the Aquitania, Donald put in. It sails at one o'clock.

Take quinine or belladonna! shouted David.

You take rat-poison! was Rilda's alternative invitation.

Midnight Blue was standing now and pouring the contents of a cocktail shaker into the grand piano.

Poor Mr. Steinway wants a drink, she explained. Not had one drink yet. Mr. Steinway. Nobody but me gives Mr. Steinway a drink.

Poor Mr. Steinway.

Sober l'il Mr. Steinway.

Le's all give Mr. Steinway a drink.

Bah, you fools! This from Simone: It's Mr. Baldwin.

Midnight Blue clambered to the top of the piano and, standing up, drew up her velvet skirt until her neat legs in their mouse-coloured stockings were exposed above the knees. She had decided apparently not to give Mr. Stein-

way any more to drink as she was pouring the contents
of the shaker through the nozzle into her own mouth. It
was sometime before she realized that she had been left
alone.

Several of the German-Americans were searching their
wraps in the corridor. Partially hidden by the hangings,
Donald Bliss stood by one of the tall windows, his arm
around Irma.

The Gräfin's screams broke in on them. As many of the
guests as remained rushed through the bedroom where the
distinguished gentleman with the sideburns snored peace-
fully on the bed, to the door of the bathroom. The tub was
full of water in which Roy Fern, fully dressed, struggled
as if he were drowning.

I drowned him, explained David, pulling the dripping
boy out of the tub, and a damned good job. My wife's
killed herself, he explained to Siegfried, who waited to
hear no more before he rushed to the bedroom window,
threw it up, to dash through the opening down the fire-
escape.

Rilda flung her arms around the Gräfin and sobbed.

Adele, she cried, he doesn't love me any more. I'm so
unhappy.

In the drawing-room window Donald pressed his lips
very closely to Irma's and whispered, Tomorrow afternoon.

Whenever you want me, she assented.

❋ *PARTIES* ❋

Alone, behind the tea-table, Fräulein Stupforsch, who had seen a good deal but who had understood nothing of what she had seen, was so terrified that she dared not make a single movement. Only her chattering teeth betrayed her abject fear.

❋ *FIVE* ❋

Rosalie Keith was celebrated for giving the worst parties in New York, but despite this undesirable reputation she never ceased giving them and people continued to go to them. It is impossible to persuade people not to go to a party in New York, particularly if they are uninvited and English. In some respects Rosalie's habits were of utility to her friends. She was a positive boon to those Americans who periodically receive letters from their English friends begging them to look after *their* English friends visiting in New York. These letters usually included a broad hint that the visitors should be escorted to Harlem, about which they had heard so much from the English visitors who had been here the preceding years. Rosalie Keith's house was not in Harlem, certainly, but enough Negroes often congregated in her drawing-room to persuade one unacquainted with the actual locality to believe that it was.

Rosalie Keith was abnormally tall, handsome, and sturdy. Her hair, prematurely white, for she was just past thirty-five, was always attractively groomed and contrasted picturesquely with her brown eyes, which were set a trifle too closely together. In evening dress, Rosalie was deceptively athletic looking, while in tweeds she resembled an indoors person badly dressed. Usually her gowns were too long or too short or too brightly coloured or too dull. Sometimes she was months behind the actual style, sometimes a few weeks ahead: she was one of those women who are never really chic.

Her marriage with a member of the distinguished Keith family had lifted her from comparative obscurity and habitual poverty into the search-light of attention and to a plane of affluence. The fact that she had divorced Cedric Keith the year after she married him only served to add to her lustre. Even the tabloids treated her respectfully. When the crash came — the papers were signed in Paris — she managed to bag a house and a suitable income for its up-keep which served her excellently in her vaulting ambition to entertain, an ambition complicated in her mind with the desire to remarry, or at the very least to have an affair which would set the whole town talking. There were those who found Rosalie middle-class and indeed there was always something extremely respectable about her sporadic attempts at unconventionality.

If Rosalie were not clever, she was neither ill-tempered nor unattractive. She seldom argued and almost as seldom actually agreed outright with any statement whatever. Her method in conversation was to smile pleasantly, if somewhat inanely, and then to utter some discreet commonplace, often quite beside the point. To those hitherto unacquainted with Rosalie, this technic was likely to prove disturbing. However maddening her intimates found her,

they tried philosophically to overlook her mental de-
ficiencies.

Rosalie Keith lived in the East Thirties in an old house
remodelled in what is so quaintly termed the " modern "
style, with electric lights embedded in Lalique vases, Cir-
cassian walnut shelves on various levels tricked out with
puppets from Copenhagen and the Wiener Werkstätte,
Madagascar birds fashioned from horn, and jade and rose
quartz figures from the Orient, vitrines set in the wall
harbouring Venetian glass animals, and divans and chairs
upholstered with materials that bore some faint, meretri-
cious resemblance to paintings in the manner of Picasso.
This house should have proved a good enough setting for a
party, but Rosalie gave far too many parties to permit herself to be self-conscious in regard to them. Nor, considering
the fact that people continued to attend them, could she
be blamed for regarding her parties as successful. Nevertheless, there were many causes for complaint and many
complaints, few of which, to be sure, ever reached Rosalie's
ears. With plenty of money at her disposal she considered
it vulgar to flaunt it in the faces of her guests, so that
sometimes when one was longing for supper, surprisingly
none was served, and, even had supper been prepared, it is
unlikely there would have been any one to serve it, as she
was accustomed to send her servants to bed directly after
dinner. On many such an occasion, visiting Englishmen
on taking their departure were obliged to spend several

nickels in a nearby drug-store telephone booth before they were able to dig up a hostess willing to give them something to eat. On the other hand, there was usually plenty to drink, if you could find a clean glass to drink it in, and knew how to chop ice.

Why anybody attended Rosalie's parties was a mystery, made still more mysterious by the conversation that preceded and followed one.

Are you going to Rosalie Keith's terrible party tonight? some one was sure to inquire, and the reply would be, I suppose so. Wasn't the one last week awful!

Latterly Rosalie had manifested the deepest interest in David Westlake, inviting him to all her dinners and if he came, attempting to usurp his attention. David was usually drunk when he arrived and always drunk when he went away, but this made him more elusive and actually added, so Rosalie believed, to his charm. She completely and conveniently ignored the existence of Rilda and never invited her with her husband. Apparently oblivious to this condition, Rilda appeared at Rosalie's table as often as she wanted to. David was often too drunk to know why he went, but sometimes he was sober enough to think it was to annoy Rilda. His invitation, of course, was permanent and anything so easy to do is generally frequently done. Besides Rosalie often made a special effort to collect David at a cocktail party and to take him home with her. It also must be remembered that if Rosalie were a poor hostess, her guests, at least, were sometimes amusing.

Two or three nights after the Gräfin's cocktail party, David was again dining at Rosalie's. Those little mischances which now and again happen to dinner parties invariably happened at Rosalie's. So, on this occasion, Simone Fly had telephoned at the last minute to ask if she might bring two charming Englishmen who had only arrived last week on the Berengaria, and Rilda, too, had decided to come. As she ignored the fact that she had not been invited, so did Rosalie resolutely ignore her presence, after she had condescended, as she had so often before, to request the butler to lay another plate.

Since his flight by the fire-escape Rilda had pretty much forgotten the existence of her young Siegfried. She certainly had not kept the rendezvous on the bear-skin rug. She was not, however, wholly unprepared, or exaggeratedly surprised, by his appearance at this dinner. Rosalie might have heard something and she had a way of doing what was expected of her. The other guests were the aforesaid Englishmen, Harry Talbot and Peter Rokeby, David and Hamish, Noma Ridge, a young English girl with dimpled, rosy cheeks who did not drink or smoke, but who atoned for the lack of these semi-precious vices by describing in an endless monotone the various forms of her amorous transports and the characteristics of the persons with whom she enjoyed them, Claire Madrilena, the Peruvian contralto, who ate so much that one wondered how she could find the time to be witty, and Simone Fly, in pale green satin, with stockings of raspberry pink, and slippers of Chinese vermilion.

The Englishmen, whom Rosalie had unselfishly seated to her right and at her left, were proving a trifle difficult.

Have you seen Pink Roses? Rosalie demanded conversationally of Peter Rokeby, whose face was as stolid as those painted on the hat-stands one observes in Paris show-windows.

Oh, yes, I think we did see that, didn't we Harry?

I think so, Peter. It was the show with the Tiller girls.

Oh, yes. There were dancing girls. What a frightful bore.

Frightful, echoed Harry, not without an effort.

Your New York is all so frightfully boring except Harlem, Peter Rokeby went on. Don't you think so, Mrs. Keith?

Rosalie smiled and replied, I do hope you are having a good time here.

And at least it's different from Mayfair, drawled Noma. You can't be a good bore there. There's too much competition.

I went to Isabel Pollanger's the other night, Claire Madrilena was explaining to David, to hear Virgil Thomson's new opera with words by Gertrude Stein. It is called Four Saints in Three Acts and I was so thrilled by it that on the way home I said to the banker who had taken me that a performance of this work would end all opera, just as Picasso with his imagination had put a stop to repetition in painting. My rich escort looked at me in consternation and exclaimed, End all opera! What would I do Thursday nights?

That must have been Charles Kilgore, David retorted laughing.

The Peruvian contralto expanded, so to speak, like a peacock raising his tail-feathers. No, it wasn't. I've seen him though, quite recently, with Midnight Blue. What a character that girl is! She takes off her drawers mentally when she talks.

She takes off her drawers literally when she doesn't talk, said David.

You're all so damned obsolete, cried Simone. Nobody wears drawers nowadays.

You must have been reading the Ladies Almanac, suggested Noma.

Simone returned to her conversation with Hamish, and Claire remarked a little more loudly than David's hearing demanded, I never sin for pleasure or profit.

Come now, urged David.

As the talk grew more animated between the various couples Rilda said to Siegfried: I really came to see you to-night. I wasn't even invited.

How did you get yourself placed next to me?

I wasn't. Why did you run away the other day?

I don't know. I was terrified. I don't ever seem to grow accustomed to New York life. It seems to go faster and faster.

Nothing goes on at all, Rilda assured him a little fiercely as she regarded him intensely with her grey-green eyes. Nothing whatever. Just parties, that's all. The only happy people left in New York are the Lesbians and pederasts, and they are so happy they are miserable. Nobody else has anything.

Take your eyes off your wife, Claire adjured David. It's quite obscene the way you stare at her. You appear to be undressing her.

David smiled as he returned his gaze to Claire.

It is very easy to look at *you,* he said.

They really didn't know what to do, Harry Talbot was saying to Rosalie, who was watching David. You see these friends of mine were at St. Moritz for the winter sports and the Crown Prince of Germany was there and they didn't know whether to cut him or not.

On account of the war, you know, explained Peter.

Did they know him? David, who had been listening, suddenly demanded.

Oh, I don't think they could have done, Harry replied.

I really had a desire for you the other night, at least I think I did, Rilda was saying to Siegfried, but you refused to give yourself till tea was served . . .

Rilda!

And you were the only sober man I'd seen in ages.

Rilda!

Are you sober tonight? Rilda adjusted the camellias at her waist and nervously twirled her champagne glass between her thumb and finger until the butler filled it again.

As Siegfried replied, Of course I am, Rilda, Claire Madrilena turned to talk with him.

I woke up in the morning with a start to see a blond head on my pillow, Noma was saying to David. I was so amazed, she continued in her baby voice. Je croyais que c'était un Nègre. I never sleep twice with the same person any more and I have such a frightful memory, she went on.

Well, you're not going to sleep with me, even once, David assured her as he viciously attacked a stuffed artichoke. I shall see to that.

My dear David, I don't like to talk about such things until I have done them, but some day — you will never know exactly how — you will find yourself in my bed, or me in yours.

Too jolly drunk to do *you* much good, David retorted as he stared furiously at Rilda, who now, however, was talking to Hamish.

Simone, waving a fork graphically in the air, exhibited her silvered finger nails, and said to no one in particular: I think deep red finger nails are very vulgar.

❋ PARTIES ❋

David, Rosalie, tired of the Englishmen, deciding to make a diversion, pleaded across the table with her most sympathetic voice, David, will you please put on a Tauber record.

Which one?

Oh, any one.

Die schönsten Augen hat meine Frau?

If you like, she replied petulantly, but I should prefer Liebe, goldener Traum.

David turned to the butler. Put a Tauber record on, he said, when you get a minute, will you, Parkinson.

Very good, sir.

Nothing ever came of this request.

David stared very hard at Rilda again, but he did not know that she was saying to her German, I shall scream if you speak of tea again. Ask me to come to see you all you like, but please do not speak of tea. We symbolically disposed of that idea when we dumped a ship-load of it into the Boston harbour.

Do you know, Peter Rokeby was remarking to Rosalie, I have nowhere to lunch tomorrow. I shall positively be hungry.

No more have I, his friend echoed.

Why don't you come here? Rosalie invited.

Thanks, we'd love to if nothing better turns up, Peter replied.

One o'clock, announced Rosalie.

That's a trifle early, Harry complained. You know we are going to that cocktail party at noon, he reminded Peter.

Oh, so we are. . . Peter turned to Rosalie. . . I think we'll pop in at a quarter to two, if you don't mind. That'll be about right for us.

Let's go to Harlem! Simone suggested, scratching her head with a dessert spoon. Blaaa!

At this moment there was an interruption. The butler leaned over the back of Rosalie's chair and whispered a few words in her ear.

It's Donald Bliss, she explained to David. . . He wants to speak to you. . . Rosalie seemed puzzled.

Where is he? David inquired.

In the drawing-room.

All right. . . David staggered out.

It's damned vulgar, that's what it is, Simone cried. Donald follows us everywhere. I saw him the other night at Noma's.

What a bloody lie! Noma protested.

Aw, shut up. . . Simone contorted her white and green face into the tortured resemblance of a martyr by fire.

It won't be a bloody lie next week, I dare say, suggested Claire.

That's different, responded Noma, now completely mollified.

✳ *PARTIES* ✳

What do you suppose he can want of David? Rosalie demanded.

Haven't the least idea. . . Rilda flared. . . Why should you care?

Let's go to Harlem, Simone reiterated. Blaaa!

We are obliged to go away directly after dinner, Peter Rokeby was explaining to her.

But you came with me, Simone complained. I'm not going home alone. Besides we're all going to Harlem.

Sorry, Mrs. Fly, we told you we had nowhere to dine. We have long had an engagement after dinner. We are going to the theatre and supper in a party with the Gräfin von Pulmernl und Stilzernl.

I want to meet her, said Noma. I hear that her parties are really amusing.

That one! Simone cocked an eye, stuck out her tongue, and rolled her head from side to side. You'll meet her in a sewer some day. So you prefer her to me! she shouted at Peter. I don't care. I'm going to Harlem. Who wants to go to Harlem?

No one accepted this invitation, but David returned to the room leading Donald Bliss in his overcoat, hat in hand.

I'm going out with Donald, David announced to Rosalie.

But David, dinner isn't over, protested Rosalie, rising.

David stood perfectly quietly against the wall by the

door leading to the drawing-room, while Donald shook hands with several of his friends and customers.

You damned swine! cried Rilda, suddenly hurling her champagne glass at David. As usual, her aim was bad, and the glass was shattered against the wall.

David, very pale, retorted, I guess it's about time I was leaving, Rilda.

You sit down, David! cried Simone. Blaaa! She pulled back her dress and began to scratch one of her raspberry knees.

Donald and I are going out, David repeated doggedly.

What's happened, David? Hamish inquired.

A pretty bloody awful thing, David replied. The champagne's run out.

But Donald was to bring some more, Rosalie explained. Still standing, she pressed her serviette against her chest, as if to soothe a pain in her heart.

That's just the trouble, Donald said. I'm sorry. I couldn't find you any more tonight.

Oh, well then, cried Simone, smoothing out her skirt, let's go to Harlem. We've got to have something to drink, you know, she explained reproachfully to Rosalie.

The two young Englishmen rose ceremoniously.

Very sorry, Mrs. Keith, Peter Rokeby said, but we must join the Gräfin. We'll drop in for lunch tomorrow, about a quarter to two, I think you said.

But David, you can't leave now before dinner is over, protested the bewildered Rosalie.

David's reply to this was to depart with Hamish and Donald, but Rilda replied, It had jolly well better be over soon. . . Come along, she said gruffly to Siegfried.

But . . .

I said, Come along! she repeated sternly.

As he followed her out, he upset his chair.

Really, Rosalie, I'm surprised at you, whined Simone. I could have called my bootlegger, she added, as she tottered out of the door.

Well, I call it beastly rude of them, said Noma Ridge.

So do I, echoed Claire Madrilena, as she helped herself to a slice of beef and a large portion of Yorkshire pudding.

Rosalie sighed.

Perhaps he'll come back tomorrow, she whispered consolingly to herself.

Parkinson continued to serve the dinner imperturbably.

SIX

In Rilda's bedroom, David lay nude on his belly in a splash of sunlight which mottled his body until it resembled a painting by Monet. Idly kicking his heels in the air, he played with a flexible brass fish while Rilda in a lace dressing-gown sipped her coffee and smoked a cigarette. A copy of the New York Times was spread out, unread, at her feet. Outside there was a prodigious honking of motor-horns and the hammering of a riveter as it flattened the headless ends of bolts in a steel construction across the way. Through the window men, poised perilously at a high altitude on the cross-beams, might be observed catching these bolts as they were tossed molten from the furnace. David glanced upwards occasionally to watch these operations.

Of course, I haven't lost everything, he said after a long silence, but it will make quite a dent in our income. I wouldn't have lost anything if my broker hadn't asked my advice. I was a fool to give it to him.

Rilda regarded her husband with an expression denoting complete infatuation.

I wonder why I adore you so, David: you're really such a bastard.

I suspect it's because I'm so swell, David replied complacently.

❋ *PARTIES* ❋

You *are* swell, David, when you are sober.

Snap out of it Rilda. . . David was scowling. . . You know damned well if you didn't love me when I was drunk, you wouldn't have much chance to love me at all. I love *you* when you are drunk, Rilda, and I think I'm a little jealous of that German.

What about Noma Ridge? Do I have to put up with that?

Don't be ridiculous, Rilda. Noma belongs to the town, to the country, in fact. She is really " America's sweetheart."

And Rosalie . . .

I can't think how you do it!

Yes, Rosalie. You certainly cannot imagine it gives me pleasure to dine with that bitch.

After all, you're never asked.

Whither thou goest . . .

Yes, we have to do that, don't we? David demanded, wriggling his great toes and wrinkling his nose. He was staring very hard at the painting of a farmhouse in the snow by Charles Burchfield, as if he were seeing it for the first time. . . Aside from our boozing, it's the worst thing about us, our damned faithfulness to each other.

Rilda laughed, a little bitterly. Our damned faithfulness, as you call it, our " clean " fidelity, doesn't get us very far, she replied. We follow each other around in circles, loving and hating and wounding. We're both so sadistic. It's really too bad one of us isn't a masochist.

I *am* a masochist, David boasted. I love to have you hurt me.

You are certainly a liar, Rilda retorted. After a pause, she added, David, do you realize that this is the first time I've seen you alone in months?

David wriggled his great toes and watched the workmen through the window.

We are really too shy to be natural when we are alone together, he responded. We become self-conscious and talk the way they do in books — I mean in good books, of course! Running his fingers through his black curls, he inquired casually: Rilda, what *do* you see in that Siegfried person? I suspect it's his name, he added.

What do *you* see in Rosalie? Why do you spend all your time in Harlem with dope-addicts and bootleggers? I'll quit if you quit.

I don't want to quit, David replied grimly. Tired of the fish, he cast it aside.

Darling, I don't mind anything so long as I am with you, Rilda assured him, but when you float off on one of those long, vague, dangerous drunks when you don't know where you are or what you are or with whom you are, I worry.

You call up Hamish, David frowned.

I call up Hamish, she admitted.

And Donald . . .

And Donald.

You go to Rosalie's for dinner, where you are not invited, and the Gräfin's for cocktails and you behave outrageously with a young blond with the incredible name of Siegfried. *I do not like it.*

No more do I, you silly.

Rilda, what do you think of the Gräfin?

I think she is a swell person. I can't help liking the Gräfin. She is so simple and so direct and it's so wonderful of her to know what she really wants.

And to get it, too, David reflected aloud. I wonder if she is amusing us or we are amusing her.

Both, of course.

There was silence for a moment. Presently David began tentatively, and he was speaking very seriously, Rilda, do you know what I think?

What? Rising, she crossed the room and, seating herself on a cushion by his side, began to stroke his back.

He went on talking: I think it is time we separated.

Separated! . . . Slipping her hand through his hair, she gave his black curls a sudden tug. . . Why, David, I couldn't live without you!

Vos beaux yeux vont pleurer. That's just the trouble. You know that song of Jimmie Durante's: I go my way and you go my way.

❄ *PARTIES* ❄

Parties! Parties! If I didn't go your way I'd never see you. Why won't you stay home occasionally?

I am home, but it's the same thing. We're shy and self-conscious, and faithful. It's this damned faithfulness that's the trouble, Rilda. We've got to get over this damned faithfulness. It's killing us. It's tearing us apart.

This " clean " fidelity. Parties! Parties!

Rilda, David announced with determination. I'm going somewhere. I think it will be London, he added, I'm so sick of seeing Englishmen.

It's no time of year to go to London. It's so foggy and cold and you're always undressing. You'll catch pneumonia and pleurisy . . .

And psittacosis? Not with the amount of Scotch I'll inhale.

You don't actually intend to go, David?

He sat up to face her, doubling his knees under him.

I *do* actually mean it, Rilda. I want to get away. No-body we know does anything but drink in this crazy town. I'm bored. If you go with me there'll be the same strain, the same pull between us . . .

Rilda looked very cold and hard. . . I suppose you want to take Roy Fern, she said. . . She was playing with a nail-polisher.

David laughed at this. That funny little rotter! he replied. No, my dearest dear, I want to go alone. I want to get away . . .

from it all. She concluded his sentence for him. When did this plan occur to you?

Weeks ago.

At a party, I suppose.

Well, it might have been. Or in a speakeasy. Must have been, in fact. I suppose you will say I was drunk. I was. I do all my important thinking when I'm drunk because then my thinking expresses my feeling. I wouldn't dare make a decision like this when I'm sober: I wouldn't actually know whether I felt that way or not.

What exactly is it that you want to get away from? she asked him.

From you, my dear, or from *us,* from what it is that makes us hate and love and drink, from this intensity of " clean " fidelity, as you call it. I want to be actually unfaithful to you in feeling and imagination as well as physically, so that I can return to you free. Now I am your slave. I never make a move or commit an action without considering whether it will annoy you or not. I swear that the strongest sensation I experience when I look at another woman is to wonder what effect it will have on you. That's why I get drunk so often. That's why you get drunk so often. We get drunk to forget we belong to each other and when we are drunk we remember harder than ever. We · waltz around and around like Japanese mice. Are you going to follow me to Rosalie's again tonight?

Good God, David, you can't go to that beastly woman's house again!

I promised I would.

Well, this time I won't follow you!

Brava! But it won't matter, Rilda, because you'll be there in my mind, or somewhere else with Siegfried. Don't you see what I mean, Rilda, my love? Don't you see what I mean? . . . Raising his hands to her shoulders he buried his face in the soft lace that covered her breast.

Of course, I see, David, and that is why I can't let you go. Suppose you enjoy your freedom, your mental infidelity and all the rest of it? Then you wouldn't come back at all. I couldn't bear that, David. What would I do without you?

Go on being outrageously hard and cynical with blond, mythological Germans, I suppose. . . David removed his head from Rilda's breast.

She was thoughtful.

I wouldn't do anything like that, she replied after a pause for reflection. Do you know, I don't think I'd see anybody at all.

In that case I'm sure I'd better go away.

David, if you go away I'll follow you . . .

Please, Rilda . . . He lay back on the blue carpet.

We might get a new set, was her next suggestion.

❊ *PARTIES* ❊

David's laughter momentarily drowned out the din of the riveting and the taxi horns.

Rilda, my pretty, there's no such thing as a set any more and you know it. Everybody goes everywhere. So that wouldn't help. . . I can't stand the racket any longer. I mean that in every sense. . . He waved his hand in the direction of the street noises. . . I'm going to embark on something large and important like the Bremen or the Majestic.

You sweet swine, you know how I hate the sea at this time of year.

Rilda . . . David was still very solemn . . . you are not going with me. I've got to go on my own for awhile, till I work this thing out.

Scrutinizing his face intently, she demanded, Do you really mean that, David?

Yes, he replied, but some inner necessity impelled him to go on. Do you remember, dearest Rilda, the night we spent in Granada, the flowing water, the nightingales, the green of the trees, and the blind musicians playing the music of Manuel de Falla in the garden?

Of course, David, and the blind gipsy who plucked his guitar strings and wailed of love in the street in front of the hotel, and the dog that barked all night, and the tinkling bells on the sturdy burros, and the flamencas with the red carnations stuck straight upright in their hair. I don't think I've ever been happier.

84

I want to try to recapture all that, Rilda, all that we were to each other and the sort of things we did then. I want to get all that back, Rilda.

She stooped to kiss his eyes.

I wonder . . . she began.

What?

If you can get it back by leaving me.

Dear Rilda, I am firm. I shall go away alone.

Rising from the cushion, she recrossed the room to stand by the window. The sound of the riveting had become deafening and persistent.

You're sure it isn't Noma or Rosalie . . . or Roy? she inquired, not without malice.

Almost sure, Rilda. . . David was very gentle. . . As sure as I can be. . . I wonder I've got the nerve to leave you. If I stay here any longer I won't have. I won't have a bit of character left. I'll just be a drunken jelly-fish swimming around my old ideal of you and polluting it. Yet, if I leave you, I'll worry furiously about this Siegfried person. You really don't know how jealous I can be.

I know how jealous *I* can be, Rilda replied. You don't think I would dine uninvited with that bitch Rosalie Keith unless I was pretty damned jealous, do you?

David lay on his back and stretched his arms.

We're shattered, Rilda, he said. What we need is a drink. It's pretty near lunch time. We've had too much sober sleep. We're not used to it. The sun's too bright. That riveting is like life in the trenches. What we need is a coupla sidecars.

Want to go into the bar?

No, there's sure to be somebody there. I don't feel up to the others yet.

Tossing a square of crimson velvet across her husband's recumbent figure, Rilda rang the bell.

A Negro maid opened the door.

Have we any cointreau, Edith? Rilda inquired.

I think so. I'll just have a look, the girl replied.

If there is, make some sidecars. Otherwise use the gin with five fruits, or make something out of absinthe and corn-meal. Is there any one in the bar, Edith?

Yes, the maid answered, before she left the room, Mrs. Fly and Mr. Butcher.

We'll stay here, David reaffirmed, adding, as the telephone bell tinkled, I'm not at home to anybody till I've had at least one drink.

Rilda lifted the receiver.

Hello . . . Who? . . . Oh yes . . . I don't think so. . . No, I can't today. . . Well, last night was different. Last nights are always different. . . No, I'm not going to Rosalie's. . . If you like.

She replaced the receiver.

The bloody boche, I suppose, said David, kicking his heels in the air.

Well, I'm not seeing him.

I know all about *that,* David announced. You told him to call up later. That means that after cocktails, after a few whiskies and sodas, or a bottle or two of champagne, when you are a little tighter, you will see him.

And what about you? she demanded.

I've just been admitting it, he went on. We're swine, filthy swine, and we are Japanese mice, and we are polar bears walking from one end of our cage to the other, to and fro, to and fro, all day, all week, all month, for ever to eternity. We'll be drunk pretty soon and then I'll be off to Donald's to get drunker and you'll be off with Siegfried and get drunker and we'll go to a lot of cocktail parties and then we'll all turn up for dinner at Rosalie's where you are never invited. She won't want you, and I shall hate you, but Siegfried will want you. And we'll get drunker and drunker and drift about night clubs so drunk that we won't know where we are, and then we'll go to Harlem and stay up all night and go to bed late tomorrow morning and wake up and begin it all over again.

Parties, sighed Rilda. Parties!

Edith returned with the cocktail shaker and glasses on a tray.

There was plenty of cointreau, Mrs. Westlake, she announced.

So you made sidecars, David suggested.

So I made sidecars, Edith admitted and quietly left the room.

Filling two glasses, Rilda handed one to David. Draining it at one gulp, he passed it back to be refilled.

I am going away, Rilda, he said. Then he added, *Alone*.

❋ SEVEN ❋

David's first two days on board ship were uneventful and unpleasant. The sea was very angry and the ship rolled and tossed and pitched and behaved as ships will under such conditions. Also David had been assigned to a cabin underneath the commissary department so that barrels of flour and potatoes were rolled over his head with a thunderous ferocity reminding him of the New York ashmen at work before dawn. Under these untoward conditions, David remained in bed and saw no one but his steward. Often he felt so sick that he hoped he would die. On the third day, however, he had recovered sufficiently to taste sardines and the breast of a chicken and to drink a pint of pale ale. On the fourth day he was amused to find whitebait en colère on the menu and ordered it to discover that the angry fish had been cooked swallowing its own tail.

The weather had become more propitious, the ship had ceased its troubled pitching, and David, wrapped in blankets, surveyed the elements from his deck chair. He was feeling somewhat easier, but as his physical ailments disappeared, his mental suffering became more acute. Life seemed so treacherous, so unnecessarily baffling. In order to rid himself of certain unhealthy habits, it seemed essential

that he should acquire others. Because the mountains
had not seemed favourable to his temperament and future
development he had forced himself to take up an equally
unsatisfactory residence in the valley. Leaving Rilda had
proved to be a terrible wrench, and yet that was the avowed
reason for his departure, to get away from Rilda. He was
beginning to wonder if it were the real reason or if this
separation would actually have the desired result of bringing them together again. He wondered what he really
wanted, whether he wanted Rilda or didn't want her — it
might be merely habit, he reasoned to himself, that caused
him to miss her so much — or whether everything would
be the same, or worse, if he were interested in some one
else.

I am so unfamiliar with myself when I am sober, he reflected, that I do not understand myself. I do not know
how I feel because I am accustomed to a keener, drunker
feeling, a feeling that intensifies, that makes anything so
simple as the slow glide of a bow over the responding
strings of a 'cello an experience not to be borne save with
deep suffering.

He had left behind him a desperate Rilda, a threatening
Rilda, a Rilda for whom Siegfried had become a favourite
synonym for retaliation. There was the possibility, of
course, that Rilda was actually interested in Siegfried, but,
after reflection, David dismissed this theory. It was incredible that Rilda could love any one but him, David.

⁂ *PARTIES* ⁂

Certainly it was not probable that she should prefer this inane, blond male even as contrast. . .

Drawing the blanket more closely under his chin, he became aware that a few valiant human beings were striding back and forth on the deck with an unpleasant display of surplus energy: corpulent men of affairs in their heavy overcoats, their wives encased in form-destroying mink, and smarter, more slender women who had braved the nipping air with no more protection than a jersey afforded.

What am I going to do? David asked himself presently, more lazily. Have I stopped drinking so that I may capture some feeling out of thought, or shall I drink again to capture thought out of feeling? How exactly should I behave as a sober person? Shall I visit the National and the Tate Galleries in London or shall I make excursions to Hampton Court and Windsor? Shall I shop at Selfridge's and eat shell-fish at Scott's and inspect the Tower?

Momentarily interrupting these vague, interrogatory reflections, he claimed a cup of bouillon from the deck steward and after drinking this, inclined to feel drowsy, he permitted himself to doze, awakening some moments later to hear a lady's voice inquire: I beg your pardon, but do you happen to speak French? I want to know the meaning of a phrase.

The lady spoke these words so distinctly that he judged she had spoken them before to sleepier ears and had repeated them in a more aggressive tone. Turning his head, he looked into the eyes of an extremely pretty girl who must have seated herself in the adjoining chair while he was asleep. Wrapped quite to her chin in a broadtail cloak, her blanket thrown carelessly across her knees, her gloved fingers clasped an unopened novel.

Why yes, David replied, I speak some French. What is the phrase?

The phrase? Oh, she exclaimed, I seem to have lost my place. I really can't remember.

In that case I'm sorry I can be of no assistance to you, David said a trifle gruffly and, settling back into his chair, he dozed once more. Indeed, he now fell fast asleep and dreamed that a blond German in silver armour was abducting Rilda with an enormous pair of sugar-tongs. Rilda was biting and scratching, but it was also apparent that she did not feel too sorry to go.

Once again he was awakened, more suddenly and violently this time, by a swift impact. His regained consciousness made him aware that his pretty neighbour was sitting on his knee with her arms about his neck.

I am so ashamed, she explained, but there *is* such a sea. I was trying to walk a little.

She made a feeble, but quite unsuccessful, effort to extricate herself from her pleasant position.

I should rise to bow, if it were possible, David remarked gallantly. Of himself he demanded: What does this mean?

If I were drunk I should know exactly how to behave. Didn't I come away to get rid of this sort of thing? Anyway, she is very pretty.

I like people of instinct and passion, the girl remarked presently.

David did not reply.

My husband, she continued, apparently apropos of nothing at all, is an old meringue.

Indeed?

I'm telling you.

Now she efficiently coped with the difficulties of getting out of David's lap, and seated herself once more in her own chair. David perceived that none of the few other deck-walkers appeared to be falling into other persons' chairs. The sea, indeed, had assumed a comparatively smooth surface.

In the circumstances he found it quite apposite to inquire: Did you find that French phrase?

Don't be funny, she adjured him without smiling. I am going to Paris to get a divorce, she added.

I am going to London, was all that David could think of to say.

That doesn't interest me at all, the girl replied. I have never exactly loved my husband, she went on after a slight pause, but when I married him I respected him. Even that respect has gone now. I have not deserved the treatment I have received.

David blew his nose violently and tucked his chin further under the blanket.

My husband has behaved like a beast. There was no course open to me but divorce and that is the course I am following.

Most comprehensible, I am sure, was David's comment, reflecting that confessions gave the confessor more pleasure than the listener. Is your husband's name Siegfried by any chance? he inquired casually.

It certainly is not, she replied indignantly. If you had looked on the passenger list you would know that my name is Mrs. Alonzo W. Syreno.

Pardon me, but why would you expect me to know that?

She regarded him with very real astonishment. You must have seen my picture in the New York papers! she exclaimed.

I have not had that honour. I have not even enjoyed the pleasure of seeing you until you began to ask me questions about foreign languages.

Her amazement certainly was not feigned.

Where have you been? she demanded wonderingly.

In New York, but you must remember I have been much too drunk to read the newspapers for the last five years.

Well, it all happened in New York, mostly on Park

Avenue. I am known as the baby wife of Alonzo W. Syreno, the radish king . . .

The . . . ?

Really, it must be true you don't read the papers. I said the radish king. He's as well known as . . . apparently she could not think of a suitably significant comparison and concluded lightly with, Oh well, anybody you can think of. He married me when I was nineteen, brought me to Park Avenue to play with his money and . . . It seemed a grand thing to do at the time, but I paid for it.

It's always the woman . . . David began sardonically.

I know, she interrupted him severely. You do say the silliest things. Well, three weeks after I married him he locked me up. It was his jealousy. His cursèd jealousy.

David lighted a cigarette with what nonchalance he could assume.

Pardon me, he demanded of his fair companion, but do you think I'm drunk?

Certainly I don't, she responded vehemently, but I wouldn't care if you were. It wasn't drunkenness that I resented in Mr. Syreno. It was his violent temper brought about by his unreasoning jealousy. I couldn't look at another man or speak to him . . . even if I'd never met him before . . . without awakening his anger. Why, one day he locked me in the preserve-closet. If it hadn't been for the milkman I'd be there yet. Have you ever been locked up?

I don't know. I don't think so. What was the milkman doing in the preserve-closet?

You do ask the silliest questions. I wish you'd let me tell this story in my own way. It's my story and I know how to tell it. Her tone was a reproof.

I'll try to let you, he said. Why are you going to Paris for your divorce?

It was an idea of Mr. Syreno's. He seemed to think it would be better that way. He gave me an awful lot of money to go to Paris with. Of course, she added, Mr. Syreno doesn't want me to get a divorce at all, and maybe I won't, she whispered, Mr. . . ?

Westlake, David informed her.

Mr. Westlake, where do you sit in the dining-room?

I haven't been in the dining-room yet, I've taken my meals in my cabin, such as they've been.

Oh, I didn't know you could do that. Well, now that you are well enough to come down, I hope you will sit at my table. I'm just a little lonely. All the other gentlemen on this boat seem to have brought their wives along. Mr. Westlake, are you married?

Oh yes, I'm married. Automatically, a tinge of bitterness coloured David's tone.

Mr. Westlake, are you happily married?

I suppose I am.

Then why, Mr. Westlake, did you mention the name of Siegfried?

David brightened perceptibly. I think, he said, we need a drink.

I think so too, Mrs. Alonzo W. Syreno replied demurely. I haven't even seen the bar yet. I don't think it would look well for a lady to go into the bar alone, do you?

You don't have to, David assured her.

Rising, she took his arm and they strolled along the deck in the proper direction. David became aware, and it hardened him, of the contemptuous stares of his fellow-passengers. Apparently his companion was unpopular.

Do you know, Mr. Westlake, until I married Mr. Syreno I had never touched a drop of hard liquor. My mother has always been very particular. I was carefully brought up all right.

I'm sure you were, David assented grimly. You touch it now, don't you? he inquired.

Oh yes, I touch it now, she responded eagerly. Mr. Syreno used to take me to night-clubs and I sat up till dawn drinking. It's a wonder I've got any looks left. Mother . . .

Where is your mother?

Mama's in Texas. Mrs. Syreno's face assumed an expression of suspicion.

Why didn't she come with you?

Why, you see mama's married again to a gentleman that runs horses, and besides I wasn't so crazy about mama coming with me. In fact I don't think I ever considered it. You see, she explained, gripping David's arm very tightly, now I'm a married woman and don't need a chaperon. Mama's a terrible bother, always telling me what to do. In her way she's just as bad as Mr. Syreno, but there are some things about Mr. Syreno that make him a little worse. For instance . . .

They were entering the smoking-room and David led her to a table in a secluded corner and rang the bell.

Do you think you could drink a double sidecar? he inquired.

Oh yes, Mr. Westlake, I could. I love sidecars. What's a double one?

You'll find out. Give us four double sidecars, David suggested to the waiting steward.

Four!

I'll drink three, he explained savagely. Why didn't you go to Reno for your divorce? he demanded.

Well now you know Paris is better to go to than Reno. Besides, Mr. Syreno would never have given me all this money to go to Reno. Why don't you come to Paris, too?

Say, what do you see in me? I'm not a radish king. I'm not even rich like your Mr. Alonzo W. Syreno. I have a devilishly mean disposition and people named Siegfried make me snort.

David drained a double sidecar at one gulp.

I don't believe I like people named Siegfried either, Mrs. Alonzo W. Syreno mused. Indeed, to tell you the truth, I don't think I ever met one, but I know what I see in you. You are the handsomest single man on the boat.

You said I was the *only* single man on the boat. David disposed of a second double sidecar.

Did I? Well, maybe you are. Then I see that too.

You'd better bring a pitcherful of sidecars, David advised the steward, a water-pitcher, not a cream-pitcher.

You do lap 'em up. Do you think it's good for you? asked Mrs. Syreno, as she finished her first.

David did not reply immediately. A couple had just sat down at a table across the floor. The lady was Midnight Blue.

Well, I'll be damned, was his audible manner of recognizing the fact.

What's the matter? inquired Mrs. Syreno. Oh, that movie star. She's swishing and swashing all over the boat. Do you know her?

Yes, I know her, said David.

To hell with her, cried Mrs. Alonzo W. Syreno, attacking another sidecar. You stick with me.

David for the moment followed her advice, but Mrs. Syreno did not appear to be a suitable person to stick to. Shortly, she was quite unfit for lunch and, after an hour's intensive drinking of sidecars, she became violently ill and was put to bed, not unwillingly, by two stewardesses.

David sat on in the smoking-room, drinking steadily and musing on his grievances. Midnight Blue still occupied a table across the floor, but she was seated with her back towards him and it was apparent that she had not yet seen him. She was engaged in an audible and innocent conversation with a man David recognized as a prominent New York banker. However, Midnight Blue was not one of David's grievances and it was not of her he was thinking when he muttered to himself, but without much conviction: The damned bitch! A little later he was inspired with a better idea. When the steward returned with a new order of sidecars he said, Have 'em turn the damned boat about. I'm going back. Changed my mind, he added feebly.

Very good, sir, replied the steward.

I'm going back, David repeated sternly. Then, Bring me a wireless blank. Bring me two wireless blanks. Bring me a dozen wireless blanks, was his eventual decision.

He consumed the few moments he had to wait for these by drinking more sidecars, and when the blanks were placed on the table before him he immediately began to write with the stub of a pencil he had borrowed from the steward. The first, addressed to Rilda, read: Coming back to kill Siegfried. Another, addressed to Rosalie Keith: Will join you at dinner tomorrow. A third, inscribed to

❋ *PARTIES* ❋

Roy Fern: Plans changed stop meet me in London on next boat. The fourth, to Hamish: If you hear anything about me don't believe it stop pay Roy's passage stop will be back in New York tomorrow stop will meet you at Rosalie's after I've killed Siegfried stop kissing parrots.

The last line put him in an idiotically good humour.

Here, he said, grinning at the steward, send these.

Very good, sir.

Did you advise the captain to put the ship about?

Yes sir.

Good. How's Mrs. Alonzo W. Syreno? . . . He must remember to find out her own Christian name.

Very sick, sir.

Good.

After drinking two more mammoth sidecars, David lunged across the room, to catch hold of the back of Midnight's chair, almost pulling it from under her. Her escort rose, snorting to protest, but Midnight turning and recognizing David, rose to embrace him.

David! she exclaimed. How swell! Didn't know you were on board. Where you been?

On a sidecar with Mrs. Alonzo W. Syreno. Know her?

Do I? She's been trying to make Charlie here. Made me feel about the size of a California oyster. Oh, by the way, this is Mr. Kilgore, Mr. Westlake. In other words, Dave meet Charlie.

The men shook hands. There was still a glare of

resentment in Charles Kilgore's eyes, and as David looked at him he seemed to grow fatter by the second, very inflated indeed in his tweeds. His face was florid and he was drinking whisky and soda.

Where are you going, Dave? Midnight Blue demanded affectionately, after they had all seated themselves.

Haven't an idea. Whither thou goest . . .

I know. I *know,* Midnight assented dryly. Well, Charlie and I are booked for Nice. It would be a pleasure to have David along, wouldn't it, Charlie?

I guess so, Charlie responded, grinning feebly and clutching his whisky and soda as if he were fearful somebody was going to snatch it away from him, but you're dead wrong about Mrs. Alonzo W. . . .

Now, that will do Charlie. I saw her.

Charlie was pathetic and a trifle bald.

What about lunch? he inquired reticently.

Lunch! cried Midnight impatiently. What we need is more sidecars, don't we, David?

Aren't we all? David demanded, smiling broadly. Aren't we all? he repeated vacuously. How's your left bank? he demanded of Midnight quite unexpectedly.

Well, you'd think it was all right if you didn't have to ask me about it, the moving picture star replied with a most engaging smile.

I want you to show me the whole damned city, David continued.

✳ *PARTIES* ✳

We might have some sandwiches here, Charles Kilgore suggested.

Now, Charlie, you speak wisdom, said Midnight. I can understand that kind of Polish. Let's have flocks of caviar sandwiches . . .

On rye bread, suggested David.

On Boston brown bread, the star gaily contradicted.

On toast Melba for me, whined Charlie.

Well, they're all for you, so why don't we order all of 'em on toast, said Midnight. In fact, Charlie, since you are so hungry, why don't you go down to lunch? I just heard the second bugle. I'm not hungry myself. Couldn't eat a thing except the lemon juice in this sidecar.

Charlie, it was evident, abhorred the idea of leaving Midnight behind, but the thought of crêpes Suzette and the other delicacies to be had for the asking in the dining-room proved too strong a temptation.

I won't be away long, Midnight, he promised, before he left the table.

Don't hurry, darling, Midnight shouted after him. Remember your indigestion. Now, my dear . . . she turned her attention to David. . . I never allow anything but silk and flesh to touch my body. Do we or don't we?

I guess we do, all right, David replied, not without enthusiasm.

Then you follow me at once, she suggested. Charlie's a

heavy eater, but even the heaviest eater winds somewhere safe to the sea.

David blinked rapidly. I've heard that somewhere, he remarked.

As they passed through the salon a lady with a shrill soprano voice was acidly executing Manuel de Falla's Seguidilla Murciana, accompanying herself on the piano with flowery cascades of false notes.

❊ *EIGHT* ❊

On a gloomy winter afternoon David was lying in the bedroom of his London hotel suite. Bright coals gleamed in the fireplace and bowls of white and red roses stood on the mantelpiece and on the dressing-table. David reflected on the ingenuity of the housekeeper who had introduced the roses while he was asleep. Outside, a deep yellow fog obscured the view and the damp vapours of the fog seeped through the cracks in the window-casement, awarding a peculiar haze to the room. It seemed neither appropriate nor necessary to David that he should get out of bed. Sipping his first whisky and soda of the day, he attempted to recall where he had been, what he had done, the night before. In respect to drink London didn't seem very different from New York except for the fact that the public places closed early so that it was advantageous to arrange to join some private party rather soon than late. He had managed, apparently without much difficulty, to join several of these parties and he remembered, with some bewilderment and not very distinctly, a succession of staircases, which duchesses ascended and descended, Venetion Negro pages carved out of wood and painted, bearing torches or trays for cards, rigid and unbending butlers, friendly   drawing-rooms,   illuminated   by   Georgian

chandeliers, with family portraits by Gainsborough and
Romney, windows hidden behind draped crimson damask,
bowls of punch, bottles of champagne, pretty actresses in
dresses that concealed their ankles and swept the thick red
carpets, groups of noble journalists with tight coat sleeves,
bowls of strawberries, ices, trifles, and fools. To one after
another of these parties he had been urged to appear by
the hosts or privileged guests. He was popular with the
English, he believed, because he was slightly eccentric.
The English prefer Americans to be eccentric: it makes
them feel more secure.

He seemed to recall a journey to the Hôtel de Paris at
Bray in a Daimler and the detail of being unable to un-
latch the outer door of a service flat on St. James's Street
and being compelled to ascend three or four flights to the
apartment he had vacated to request the owner to come
down and let him out with his key. He was not certain,
of course, that all these events had occurred during the
immediately previous night. Further, he could dimly recol-
lect a strange bedroom or two. Here his memory instructed
him but feebly. What was he doing in these beds? Whom
had he encountered there? Until he had tasted his first
whisky and soda he had felt a vague sense of shame, but
the source or cause of this was completely unknown to
him.

With his second whisky he began to realize poignantly
that he had not yet received any replies to his numerous

wireless messages and cablegrams. He was the more particularly disturbed by this fact because he could not remember very clearly what he had said in them, or to whom he had dispatched them, but he was sure that he must have sent off dozens every day. He knew, of course, that most of them must have been addressed to Rilda. Probably he had projected at least fifty messages to Rilda, but he had not received one word from her in return. It was possible she was punishing him. She had predicted that this separation would not serve to alter his conduct, and she had been right. There was no longer any reason or any logic in his movements. He could not account for his behaviour. What did he want? What was he good for? He couldn't explain. Here he was, as usual, playing havoc with his cells, drinking with passion, accepting amorous advances without too much protestation, making amorous advances with what fervour remained to him, sleeping it off, and beginning all over again the next day. The worst of it was that he liked it.

And Rilda? Did she drink because he did or did he drink because she did? This was a question they frequently propounded to each other in their shy, aggressive manner, but they never had succeeded in arriving at any satisfactory decision. Thought of Rilda — and when didn't he think of her, particularly when he was lying in another woman's arms? — always created emotion in him. Rilda was the reason for most of his acts: he was conscious in restrospect that he did everything to please her or to annoy her. And now Rilda ignored his cabled questions. The real solution, he believed, was not that she was punishing him. Rather, she was too drunk to read his messages, and much too drunk to reply to them. If she were drunk, David felt certain she would be with Siegfried: a good enough name for a dog or an opera hero, but ridiculous for a man.

The telephone bell tinkled.

Hello.

Hello. Is that you, David? The velvety voice was obscenely feminine at this hour.

Who is speaking? . . . David was quite brusque. . . Why don't you English say, Are you there? any more?

It's only the Americans who say that now. You can recognize them by it, even when their accent is excellent. We also employ the American upright telephone now and prefer it, while you have taken over our funny old instruments.

Indeed. You are very instructive today. What do you think of Stanley Baldwin and Sybil Thorndike?

Baldwin! Sybil is rather depressing, I think. She breathes so deeply. She'll be a Dame if she doesn't watch out.

Are you going to hear Paul Robeson on Sunday?

The Albert Hall is not on my street. I expect to go to Betty Chester's to hear Hutch play.

❋ *PARTIES* ❋

Well, I may see you there. Would it be asking too much to propose that you wear a blue ribbon in your hair or violets so that I shall know you.

Now, David Westlake, the owner of the voice protested, it's about time you should begin to recognize my voice. We've been together pretty constantly after all during the past week. In fact, this is about the only time we've been separated.

Just here, David emitted an ejaculation of surprise, caused by the fact that the bathroom door, which he was facing, was gradually opening. Presently a figure with untidy blonde hair, her body wrapped in a sheet, stood in the frame of the doorway.

Call me a little later, will you? David managed to stammer into the receiver before he replaced it. Then, to the apparition in the doorway: Jesus, where did *you* come from?

From the bathroom, she replied, rubbing her eyes sleepily.

Before he attacked this problem from a fresh angle, David poured out another drink for himself.

I know *that,* he cried, but, speaking generally . . . He waved his hand in the air.

What is the matter with you, David? I've been here for days . . . ever since we got off the boat. Ever since . . . her eyes lighted up as she made a feeble attempt at humour . . . we were sober. Who were you telephoning to?

I don't know. Somebody called me. I don't know who it was. You say you've been here ever since we got off the boat?

Most of the time. Why did you hang up so quickly? Afraid I'd get jealous?

Standing before the mirror of the dressing-table, she regarded herself with apparent disfavour, frowning at her image as she lighted a cigarette.

Good God, no. I told you I don't know who it was, and I certainly had no idea you were here. I hung up because I was amazed to see you come out of that bathroom. I certainly don't give a damn whether you get jealous or not.

We'll see whether you care or not, Mrs. Alonzo W. Syreno cried. If you don't behave yourself I'll get out, that's what I'll do. I'll go to Paris.

My dear lady, I don't give a damn what you do. I thought you *were* in Paris. Will you have a drink?

No thank you. Mrs. Syreno's tone was bitter as she began to gather up articles of feminine wearing-apparel from the floor. David, pouring out another drink, wonderingly observed them for the first time.

Mrs. Syreno searched the room vainly with her eyes for a second glass and finally fetched the tooth-mug from the bathroom.

I think I'll change my mind, she said.

He poured whisky and soda into the mug, while he

noted that the other bed had the air of having been occupied. A sheet was missing.

A page appeared with a telegram.

David tore it open to read: Am joining you immediately love Rilda.

I don't believe it, he cried aloud.

What is it? Mrs. Alonzo W. Syreno demanded.

By way of reply, David tossed the cablegram on the live coals in the fireplace. Now, I've *got* to be drunk, he cried. I've simply got to pull myself together and go on a serious binge. . . He poured out another whisky. . . What did we do yesterday, visit Whitehall or inspect the Wallace collection?

Mrs. Alonzo W. Syreno was obviously puzzled.

He reassured her: Well, we wouldn't know anyway.

The bell of the telephone sounded again.

Hello.

Oh, it's you, the hello girl. Well, who are you?

Mrs. Syreno, glowering, hovered close beside the instrument.

David . . . the voice was liquid and musical . . . we've been together for days and days, eternity almost, and you've forgotten the sound of my voice, my voice which you said was like trickling water, the fountains of Rome, the falls at Lodore, the mountain rivulets of Granada . . . but you will recall your pretty phrases.

❋ *PARTIES* ❋

David clapped his hand to his head. I am certainly going mad, he assured himself. Then, into the receiver, Where are you?

Downstairs. I'm coming up.

You don't know where I live.

Nonsense. You're in 46.

I'll kill myself if you come up.

Pleased to have you.

The connection was broken.

David laughed, and sang:

> Come in the evening,
> Come in the morning,
> Come when expected,
> Come without warning.

Turning to face Mrs. Alonzo W. Syreno, he realized that he was still unacquainted with her Christian name. It did not seem to be the appropriate moment to ask her to tell it to him.

She is coming up, he announced grimly.

Who is coming up? Girding the sheet more closely about her, Mrs. Syreno settled herself in an arm-chair and lighted a cigarette.

I wish I knew, David replied, and in response to a knock at the door, called out a mock-cheery, Come in.

A page opened the door for a lady enveloped in a black cloak with a white fox collar. Black hair was visible beneath her black silk hat which fitted her head like a sheath, and her black eyes seemed more prominent because she had painted her eyelids blue.

Who is this person? the newcomer demanded, levelling her black eyes on Mrs. Alonzo W. Syreno.

And who the hell are you? the American, rising, retorted.

David, quite nude as usual when he habited a bedroom, sat on his heels, glass in hand, in the middle of the bed, and commented: It might just as well be America. It couldn't be worse. Anyway, if you tell each other who you are, maybe I'll find out.

The brunette islander approached the bed.

David, she inquired, and her tone was suspiciously gentle, is this woman your wife?

David laughed hysterically. Good God, no, he cried. I never saw her before, or you either, he added, but my wife is coming. She will soon be here. Then beware. She will sweep the horizon with tear-bombs.

Mrs. Alonzo W. Syreno scowled, folded her arms, and gave an order.

David, she commanded, throw this woman out!

Before it actually happened, David reminded himself that fragile young girls were ridiculous when they played tragedy queens. Then, foreseeing a hurricane, he concealed his head beneath the sheet. Cries, screams, curses, and sobs reached his ears, the rending of cloth, and eventually a dull thud. When he found the courage to look up again he saw that Mrs. Alonzo W. Syreno was lying entirely naked on the rug in front of the fire. She was sobbing softly. The dark visitor, perfectly composed, was removing her cloak and presently stood before him in a black lace dress which swept about her feet in scallops.

Fight to the death! David urged. In America we fight to kill. You might do worse, he added, and my wife who is coming will take on the survivor. What I like is a good auto-da-fé. I wish all the rest of 'em were here to get into it: Rosalie Keith and Fougère Royale, Prince of Sweden. But, if you don't die, I hope you'll both come to my cocktail party on Friday. Nora Holt is going to sing and Hutch will play. Cocktails by Fortnum and Mason. Beds by Selfridge. Pyjamas by Sulka. . . .

David . . . the Englishwoman had seated herself on the bed, and her voice was languid . . . why did you leave me this morning? At Hyde Park Corner too! I slept on the couch in Natalie's uncomfortable Chippendale drawing-room with the servants dusting and brushing up about me, but I don't sleep there tonight. Here am I and here I stay.

You could sing that phrase, David suggested. Jerome Kern has written holy music for it. I think this whole scene would be better sung anyway, he continued.

Stroking her bruised and scratched arms, Mrs. Alonzo W. Syreno, still prone, moaned softly.

✳ *PARTIES* ✳

As for *her,* the English girl ordained, she can get dressed and go.

This whore's dead. Send up a new whore, quoted David. Are you a lion tamer, my pretty?

David, you absolutely infuriate me, the dark lady replied, rising. You know perfectly well who I am and what I am. Since you've been in London you've certainly spent enough time hanging around my flat and drinking my Scotch. You've dropped so many unextinguished cigarette ends on the cushions of my Bentley that my chauffeur tells me the car will have to be reupholstered. And you have the face to ask me who I am!

That's a lie, feebly cried the recumbent Mrs. Alonzo W. Syreno, who now managed to work herself into a sitting posture and then to her feet. He's been with me ever since he's been in London. . . She stooped to recover her now ragged sheet, and wound it about her. . . We got off at Plymouth together, she continued, and if it hadn't been for me he never would have stayed on the tender. The waves were washing high, but I held him. God, he was drunk! For Christ's sake gimme a drink, she concluded.

David considerately refilled the tooth-mug.

Well, as far as I'm concerned, he said, I don't remember any of it or who's who, or what have you. You can both stay or go or anything you please, until my wife arrives, and then probably it won't be so good for some of us. Say, are *you* married? he asked the Englishwoman who was crying a little as she stood beside the fireplace tearing the petals from a rose, one by one.

Married! I should jolly well think I am. You don't suppose I could go to other men's bedrooms unless I were married.

It was plain that she was horrified at his insinuation.

I'll bet you're married to a German, was his next thrust. I'll bet his name is Siegfried.

David held his chin very high.

He's not a German and his name is not Siegfried, the lady replied with a dangerous calm. You, as well as I, have been unfaithful to him, disloyal — bringing adultery and fornication into the home of your best friend.

My God, Hamish!

She bowed her head.

You, Irene!

She nodded.

So I came to England to give dear old Hamish horns!

Laughing bitterly, he gulped down another tumblerful of Scotch.

Oh, *you* didn't give him horns. He had nice long antlers before you arrived, Irene retorted.

But I don't remember . . .

❊ PARTIES ❊

Don't insult me, David, please.

You see, Mrs. Alonzo W. Syreno remarked complacently, it would have been better for you to stick to me.

It would have been better for me, David shouted, if I had been born impotent or made into a eunuch. I'll have it done tomorrow. I'm sick of sex . . . women anyway . . . sick of liquor, goddam sick of everything. I'm getting out.

Rising unsteadily, nude as he was, he made for a chest of drawers. He pulled the topmost of these out so forcibly that it fell to the floor and the contents, shirts, collars, handkerchiefs, and socks, were dumped out in disorder. Gathering an armful of these, he transferred them to a drawer in his Vuitton trunk. He interrupted himself long enough to call out, Come in, in reply to a knock at the door.

Let 'em all come in, he muttered. It doesn't matter now. I'm going away.

Snatching another cablegram from the page-boy, he tore it open, read the message, and handed it to Irene, explaining, It's from Hamish.

She read it aloud in some wonder: Dear David I killed Siegfried stop so did Roy stop we sail today Mauretania stop Rilda gone to San Francisco stop reserve suite at Cavendish stop notify Irene love Hamish.

✳ *PARTIES* ✳

Dear old Hamish, murmured David.

He must be crazy, cried Irene. I'm off for Madrid.

Mrs. Alonzo W. Syreno had crumpled on the floor again.

A drink! For God's sake, gimme a drink! she moaned.

❋ *NINE* ❋

On a gloomy day in Paris David hugged the warmth and snugness of the Castiglione Bar. Outside, a persistent, damp drizzle made it very chilly, but the bar was as cozy as could be. Sitting in a shadowed corner, David kept Otto busy shaking sidecars.

Aside from the bar attendants, there were three other occupants of the small room: first, a fat American gentleman who was consuming an amazing number of glasses of whisky and soda at a table near the entrance-door; second, an American lady, obviously ill at ease to find herself alone, who had ordered nothing, but from time to time consulted her watch, apparently in anxiety about the delay of some one she was expecting; third, a German, accompanied by a police dog who, head on paws, slept on the floor. It did not seem likely to David that he would become friendly with any of these persons.

Since his arrival in Paris, David, everything considered, believed that he had behaved with comparative circumspection. His reported affair with Irene, despite the fact that his memory could not supply him with a single shred of evidence in regard to it, had disturbed him. Not, he reasoned, that Hamish would care very much, even if he knew, for Hamish and Irene were through with one

another. Nevertheless, even taking it for granted that Irene
were responsible for what had happened, there was something unpleasant about the episode in retrospect. In an
effort to escape and forget, he had shaken Irene and London off and voluntarily deprived himself of the company
of Mrs. Alonzo W. Syreno — if he ever saw her again he
must remember to ask her to tell him her Christian name
— although he did not doubt she was in Paris even at the
moment and would cross his path as soon as he had im-
bibed enough liquor to forget himself.

Why, he asked himself, did he not return to New
York? He had proceeded quite far enough with this adven-
ture, experiment, whatever it might be called, to be certain
it was foredoomed to failure. Some inner urge, however,
compelled him to continue to emulate the examples of
Ulysses and the Wandering Jew, an inner urge that was
stimulated by the contradictory messages he received from
America. Was Rilda in California or was she on her way to
join him? He did not know. Nor could he be certain about
Siegfried.

While he was thus occupied with his sombre medita-
tions and a succession of sidecars which, he reflected, Otto
was an artist in shaking, he was interrupted by the American lady who was sitting at an adjoining table. That she
had become, during the last few moments, increasingly
nervous, he was aware. At last she had apparently sum-
moned sufficient courage to address him.

I beg your pardon, she demanded, in a voice which her embarrassment pitched much higher than was necessary, but are you Mr. Alonzo W. Syreno?

Before a very much astonished David had an opportunity to reply, the gentleman near the door responded, Madame, I am Mr. Alonzo W. Syreno. . . He rose and bowed. . . And you, I presume, are Miss Hortense Caldwell.

Yes. I am so sorry. . . The poor thing was more embarrassed than ever. . . How was I to know?

The fault is mine, he replied gallantly, and straightway he invited her to join him.

He had obviously made this suggestion because at his table they would be further removed from the other occupants of the bar. The lady immediately appreciated his intention and the conversation was continued in a tone inaudible to David and the German.

David had not been obliged to answer the lady's question. He had not, indeed, spoken a single word and had been completely ignored, probably overlooked, after the recognition scene. He was considerably amazed by the incident. As a matter of fact he had always regarded Mr. Alonzo W. Syreno as a legendary character and it was somewhat astonishing to have him turn into flesh and blood. The man's attention was so absorbed by his companion that David had an opportunity to observe him more closely. He was, to be sure, stout and middle-aged, but his face proclaimed character and his dress published his taste. He was slightly bald and his eyes required glasses, but these details only served to accentuate his distinction. He was certainly much more of a personality than the woman he had married. How had such a man acquired — or been willing to retain — a musical comedy name like Alonzo W. Syreno? These mental questions could neither be dismissed nor considered lightly. The German with the police dog rose, throwing down a ten franc note to pay his bill and the tip, and lumbered out just as it occurred to David to wonder if he was going to turn out to be Siegfried's brother.

Another sidecar, David ordered of Otto, as he attempted to collect his thoughts. Should he definitely approach Mr. Alonzo W. Syreno and introduce himself? I met your wife on a boat, Mr. Syreno, might be his opening speech. Or should he continue to linger in the background as a curious observer, or should he leave the bar altogether and attempt to forget the ludicrous coincidence which had brought him into the presence of this man? After he had consumed his sidecar, he decided, with some reluctance, on the latter course. Certainly, it would have been amusing to hear Mr. Alonzo W. Syreno's views of the woman who bore his name.

He waited on the wet pavement while the chasseur sought a taxi and, when one was found, directed the chauffeur to drive him to Larue's, which he felt convinced would be reasonably warm and cheerful. The servants would be polite, as well-paid and well-tipped servants usually are, and his captain would point out to him the most excellent dishes on a menu which included no errors. He considered the wine he should order: he fancied Château Margaux met his mood for the day, and if the captain's imagination failed, he determined to eat an omelette maison. He was beginning to feel exhilirated, a pleasant glow warmed his veins, a sensation that is within the reach of any one who can afford to drink the proper number of sidecars. David believed firmly, however, in the theory that there was something about the atmosphere of Paris that gave an extra tang to a sidecar, or any other drink whatever. At this moment, he was convinced, however falsely, that he would not be drunk for several hours. How swiftly his chauffeur was driving on these slippery streets! Swerving down the Boulevard past the Madeleine at terrific speed, he brought up safely before Larue's.

Warmly greeted by the chasseur, and still more warmly by the maître d'hôtel, he was presently seated with his back against one of the windows which looked out towards the Madeleine. He was feeling very contented with himself and the place — it was charming to be alone, for once — and thought it was quite likely that his luncheon would be a complete success. He had exactly reached that point in drinking where every value is enhanced.

Pour commencer, saumon fumé, he commanded, and

then he added the omelette and a bottle of Pouilly, on second thought rejecting the red wine. As he ordered the wine, he meditated on the general appearance of sommeliers, almost invariably staunch, brawny, tall fellows with strong hands and honest, kindly faces. In general, he fancied, they should be Normans. All day long they recommended wines and pulled corks, thus developing brain and muscle, and even encouraging latent faculties of imagination. David wondered what a sommelier would be like and determined to strike up an acquaintanceship with one as soon as opportunity offered.

While the waiter was serving the saumon fumé David observed Midnight Blue, very correct and sober, sitting at a table across the room with Charlie Kilgore. They saw him at almost the same instant that he became aware of their presence and they bowed, but there was something in their manner which did not make him eager to cross the floor to speak to them. Indeed, in his present state of mind he was rather annoyed to encounter Midnight and considered it a bad omen. He tasted the saumon while the sommelier twirled the bottle of Pouilly in its ice-bath.

Who was this approaching his table, a familiar face and figure, an American youth who was friend, acquaintance, enemy, something, nothing? He could not recall at the moment, but he regarded the prospective visitor in the light of an intruder and an annoyance.

❉ *PARTIES* ❉

Hello, David.

Hello. David extended his hand. The fellow was handsome in a romantic way, with light hair combed straight
back and flattened to his head with brilliantine, a pair of
startling eyes, the colour of purple pansies, warm-blooded
cheeks, and a figure that was obviously an extremely simple problem for any tailor.

David, however, was still puzzled. For all he knew this
man might be his cousin. He just couldn't remember *who*
he was and so he invited him to sit down.

Thanks, David. I've eaten a splendid lunch, but I'll
take coffee with you, if it's all the same to you.

As it appeared to be all the same to David, the waiter
altered the position of the table to permit the fellow to seat
himself on the upholstered bench beside his host.

Once comfortably installed, the man inquired. How
long you been over?

Oh, I don't know. David was vague. Days, I guess.
Weeks. A long time, he added. It seems years.

The young man seemed to be dazed. Whew! was his
astonished comment. You must be enjoying yourself.

I am, he replied solemnly. Hell, yes, I'm certainly enjoying myself.

The sommelier filled two glasses with pale gold Pouilly.

Well, here's to you! the young man cried and drained
the wine at one gulp as if it had been whisky. Seen Hamish
lately?

Suddenly David remembered. This was Hamish's friend, Buddy Parsons, who went to all first nights and débutante parties and vernissages and tried out the new speakeasies before any one knew whether they sold poison or not. He was invariably well-informed on such subjects as interested that large but special public which reads, or looks at the illustrations in, Vanity Fair and the New Yorker. David also remembered why he had forgotten his identity. Never had he, David, been even comparatively sober when he had encountered Parsons previously. Most of what he knew about him he had learned through Hamish.

Not very lately, Parsons, he replied, enjoying the bouquet of his wine and sipping it gently. Hamish is in New York or Utah or one of those places. I've only just come from London.

As the sommelier refilled Parsons's glass David advised: Better bring another bottle and put it on ice.

Bloody awful place in winter, was Parsons's comment. Worse than this. Those bleeding yellow fogs! Anyway, even if it does rain here there's the food and drink to take the curse off, but Berlin is the place. Ever been to Berlin? Parsons gulped down another glass of Pouilly.

No, I've never been in Berlin, David replied, demanding anxiously, Wouldn't you prefer a whisky and soda? That's not a very long drink you've got.

Naw . . . Parsons lifted the nearly empty bottle from the ice-pail and examined the label. . . This is one of my favourites.

Well, said David, I guess there'll be enough in the cellar. Better bring *two* more bottles, he suggested to the sommelier, who was busy twirling the second.

The man regarded him with wonder not unmixed with horror.

I'll never be able to get acquainted with *this* sommelier, David reflected.

The sommelier refilled both glasses and removed the first bottle.

Do you know Rosalie Keith? Parsons inquired and then answered his own question: Of course, you do! You're her cavaliere servente or something like that. Anyway, she gave one of the strangest dinners recently: saumon fumé — that's what reminded me — sweetbreads on toast, and vanilla ice-cream. I was so hungry when we rose from the table I excused myself and stepped right over to Reuben's.

Rosalie *is* eccentric, David admitted, wondering if this fellow was spoiling his luncheon. He took another drink while the waiter was serving the omelette.

Why, there's Midnight Blue! cried Buddy Parsons. What's she doing here with Charlie Kilgore? No good, I'll bet. I wonder how the tabloid gossips missed that bit of dirt.

They must be trying to conceal it, David commented

dryly. That's why they came to Larue's, so nobody'd see them.

Well, the food is good here and you do meet a lot of people in Paris, but give me Berlin. I like beer.

Want some? David inquired, filling Parsons's glass with wine in the temporary absence of the sommelier.

I should say not. This is my favourite wine. There's Tallulah Bankhead.

David turned to observe an animated young blonde conversing, cigarette in hand, with her companion.

Do you know Malvina Crane? Parsons inquired.

No, I don't believe I do. Do you mean the dancer?

That omelette looks swell, said Parsons. The aroma is excellent.

The taste is even better, David responded. Want some?

No thanks. I'll stick to the vino. Yes, I mean the dancer. She's here in Paris. Let's go to see her after lunch to cheer her up. She's in a bad way.

What's the trouble?

Desperately enamoured of a young gigolo back home — his name's Kim Skene — very expensive. He doesn't have affairs: he has transactions. Her father — the big gambler, you know — threatened to shoot him if she didn't give him up. So she comes over here to save her sweet man's life and sleeps all day and cries all night — in night-clubs. They put her out of Zelli's the other morning. The head-waiter complained that she was breaking the hearts of the customers.

Well, if she sleeps all day, how the hell can she see us now? Besides I don't want to see her. Why should I go out on a rainy day to look at a girl cry? I think I prefer the Rue de Lappe tonight.

The waiter was pouring out coffee. Parsons, by this time, had decided not to take any.

We'll be through here by four o'clock, he reminded David after consulting his wrist. You can't go to the Rue de Lappe at four o'clock.

David pondered this. I don't see why not, he countered. Just because nobody ever has. . .

Oh, well if you want to.

I'd just as soon make it the Bal Colonial in the Rue Blomet. I love to watch the biguine.

Can't do that. It isn't the right night. . . Parsons knew about these things.

What makes you think we'll be through at four o'clock? David demanded.

Gotta. Gotta go see Malvina cry, Parsons explained, as he poured more wine into his empty glass.

Where does she live?

Oh, one of the big hotels like the Crillon or the George V or the Edward VII. Every taxi-driver in Paris knows where Malvina lives. They *have* to. It's like going to the Opéra or the Bon Marché or the Invalides, to go see Malvina. They *have* to know where she lives.

Midnight Blue had hesitated in the doorway to speak to Tallulah Bankhead who was also leaving. The moving picture star sent David an invitation with her eyes. David recalled dimly that he was getting drunk again, as usual, he reasoned, to escape. To escape from what? Not from the louse sitting by his side. He was going on with him. Well, there was Malvina Crane to inspect, a new promised land. Mentally, he tried to evoke a picture of the dancer: a difficult process in his present state. He seemed to recall her legs, but for the life of him he could not bring back her face.

A few cognacs followed the coffee. Midnight Blue and Tallulah Bankhead had long since taken their departure. The blue Paris twilight was upon them.

Well, I guess it's time to go, Buddy Parsons announced definitively.

David's watch seemed to indicate that it was a quarter to five. After he had paid the addition and settled the pourboire accounts with his captain, his waiter, and the sommelier, they slowly and solemnly staggered out, leaving behind them five empty quart Pouilly bottles for an incredulous service to gaze at.

On the pavement, the chasseur assisted them into a cab and demanded directions.

Chez Madame Malvina Crane, was the only address Parsons gave, as he sank back against the cushions.

Entendu, monsieur, replied the chasseur, and in a few rapidly spoken words, he informed the chauffeur where to go.

When the chauffeur started off there was complete silence in the cab. After a time Buddy Parsons said: You know it's something to think about, this rain in Paris.

David, whose mind was on Rilda, replied belligerently, It's probably raining in New York, you know.

You're a sweet hell of a guy, you are! Buddy Parsons shouted in a sudden blind fury. Goddam unpatriotic, I call it, bringing up that New York rain. Why, New York . . .

Oh, shut up, cried David. Awhile ago it was Berlin. I'm sick of your flashy blubber. To think it cost me money to get *you* drunk!

Buddy Parsons tried to light a cigarette, but he could not cope with his lighter and eventually the cigarette dropped unlighted from his nervous fingers into his lap.

His lips trembled as he said, I don't know why I'm taking you to see Malvina. I don't like you. I never did.

I don't know why I'm going, David replied coldly, unless it's to annoy you.

Oh, you don't annoy me. *You* couldn't annoy me. . . Suddenly the blood suffused Parsons's face and he added savagely, You can go to Hell!

※ *PARTIES* ※

There was silence inside the car for a few moments, as the chauffeur drove swiftly over the slippery pavement, the automobile frequently skidding, causing all the chauffeurs in the vicinity excitedly to press the bulbs that sounded their sirens.

Presently Parsons, extremely sulky, spoke again. Where are we going anyway? he demanded.

To see Malvina Crane, I suppose, David replied.

To hell we are! I don't know the dame. I'm going to the Rue de Lappe. . . He pounded lustily on the window. . . Hey, you cocher, arrêtez, s'il vous plaît. Je veux descendre, descendre . . . alors, ça m'est égal.

The cab drew up to the kerb . . . they were somewhere on the Champs-Elysées, and the view of the Arc de Triomphe ahead of him symbolized to David the way he felt at the moment. . . Parsons got out with great difficulty. Then, tottering, he turned to address David.

You dirty son of a bitch, were his parting words.

The wheels were turning rapidly again, the cab was pushing forward, and he was once more on his way to Malvina Crane, whom he did not know. It would be quite simple to give an order which would change the direction of the cab, but he did not give it. Probably he was what he had been called, and more besides, he reflected without bitterness towards himself. Rosalie, Irene, Mrs. Alonzo W. Syreno — what was that woman's Christian name? —

and now Malvina. What was the matter with him? What
was it all about? What was the sense of it? Were his actions due to temperamental or biological causes? In his
present condition suitable replies to these questions did
not occur to him. Shortly, indeed, before he had time for
more reflection, even of the vague variety, he stood before
the desk of the concierge in Malvina's hotel, inquiring for
the dancer, announcing plausibly, Monsieur Westlake, de
la part de Monsieur Parsons.

It was all made easy for him. Eventually ushered into
the elevator, a little later he knocked on what proved to be
the correct door, opened it, and boldly entered Malvina
Crane's room. It was, to be exact, a bedroom. Miss Crane
had not permitted herself the luxury of an apartment. The
dancer, in an orchid négligé, turned her fluffy orange head
and looked at David with green, red-rimmed eyes. She
was sitting on one of the beds, with her back to the door,
and she held a glass in her hand. The floor was strewn with
dresses, underthings, and stockings. The tables, the dressing-table, the mantelpiece were laden with bottles, empty
and full, siphons, soda bottles, ginger ale bottles, used and
clean glasses, pitchers of orange- and lemon-juice, containers of powdered sugar, and bowls of ice, half-melted and
fresh.

Hello, she said, who are you?

David, David Westlake. Buddy Parsons asked me to
come up here and then something — not the faintest idea

what — happened in the taxi and he went somewhere else. So I came up here.

Glad. Sit down. Gotta see some one. . . Turning away from him, she poured herself a drink. . . Help yourself, she invited.

He removed his overcoat and after hanging it with his hat on the bathroom door, he staggered around among the bottles until he found some gin and orange juice. Then he sat down, in a chair near a window, facing his hostess.

Ever in love? she demanded after a pause. She was not looking at him.

Yes . . . Not so sure.

I don't mean that. I don't want you to be in love with me. That would be hopeless. . . She looked straight into David's eyes. . . I'm in love with a boy in America, Kim Skene. Perhaps you never heard of him.

Kim Skene? Sounds like something. He rolled it over, gulped down his drink, and rose unsteadily to pour himself out another.

It isn't. Not a damned thing. Just Kim Skene, Malvina replied. They made me come over here, she added. . . Great tears rolled down her cheeks.

I know, he said. Pity his name isn't Siegfried.

She did not appear to have heard this comment. I love him so much, she continued ardently. I can't live without him, but my father threatened to shoot him if I didn't

leave him, and so I came over here. I'm sorry I came. . .
She was sobbing now.

I know, he repeated. Kim Skene? Pity his name isn't
Siegfried. I'd encourage your enterprising father.

I'm awfully glad you've come, she said, wiping her eyes
and blowing her nose. I wanted somebody to talk to. Buddy
Parsons usually comes in.

Used to know him. Friend o' my friend, Hamish. Good
egg. Where is he?

I dunno.

Want to go out to dinner?

Luvvit. Can't eat a thing, but hate to stay alone. You
know how it is. . . Her hand trembled as she poured
herself another drink. . . That boy's eyes, Kim's eyes,
get between me and the food. At night they get between
me and the pillow. She began to sob audibly.

I know, David repeated. He made himself another
drink. . . Where you want to go for dinner?

Oh, I don't care. Voisin's, Larue's, some simple place.
I can't eat or drink: I'm too unhappy. I could just die, but
I like to think the food would be good if I did eat it. That
boy's eyes . . .

You miss him, don't you?

Miss him! I can't explain how much. He's so sweet, my
Kim. I should say I do. I just can't get along without him.
You see my father threatened to shoot him if I didn't come
away. So I came. I just can't eat or drink or sleep without

him. Wish I was back. Haven't had a drink since I came to Paris. Well, two . . .

Poor kid. . . Seating himself beside her on the bed, David affectionately put his arm around her shoulder. . . I'm sorry.

Her head drooped to his breast as she continued to sob softly.

What's your name? she inquired.

David Westlake. I was coming here with Buddy Parsons and he got out of the taxi: so I came on without him.

I'm expecting Buddy. Where is he?

Dunno.

Sighing, she gulped down another drink. I'm awfully unhappy, she told him. Why don't you take your coat off?

Dunno, he replied. He removed his coat and waistcoat.

What a nice shirt, she remarked, as he resumed his position beside her. I can't sleep or eat or drink. His eyes get between me and . . . Isn't your collar tight?

He loosened it.

My father threatened to shoot him, she said softly, as she slipped one hand between David's arm and his body and carried her lips upward to meet his.

His Why? was smothered by her tearful kisses.

❋ TEN ❋

The city of New York is difficult to describe or understand save in terms of paradox, and so, perhaps, it is more
satisfactory, for those who may, to instinctively feel the
metropolis rather than to attempt to comprehend her. Not
infrequently some of the balmiest days of the year there
fall in January and February. Buds are nearly ready to burst
on the boughs of the trees in the Park, and the birds are
tempted to return from the south. The temperature becomes so oppressive that electric fans and filmy garments
are sought from store-closets, but no sooner have they been
discovered than a passing and perverse breeze ushers in another week of winter. Snow or rain or sun may follow:
there is no means of determining by precedent. Some of
the coldest days in the year are likely to happen in June
or July. It is strange that Americans have never adopted
the English habit of carrying umbrellas, for New York is
quite able to produce a cloud-burst out of the sky on the
most clement day. When, however, the sun shines in New
York, be it warm or cold, the heart is happy, and it is
probable that the sun shines more often there than in any
other capital of the world.

The physical changes in this city are even more amazing than the atmospheric changes. All cities alter somewhat in the course of time, but they alter slowly. In Rome
we can follow the trend of these alterations through the

last two thousand years, a souvenir of every century remains. Mediæval Paris has entirely disappeared, and there are comparatively few traces even of the eighteenth century in modern London, but what has happened in the way of demolition and construction in these two cities has happened temperately and not unexpectedly. New York on the other hand is in a constant state of mutation. If a city conceivably may be compared to a liquid, it may be reasonably said that New York is fluid: it flows. Leave town for a week and you will notice changes when you return. It is quite possible to pay a visit to your lawyer or your bank only to discover that the erstwhile building in which their business was formerly transacted has disappeared in favour of a deep hole in the ground. Contrariwise, a new and glittering tower, fifty or more storeys in height, may rise in another direction before you are aware of the preparatory excavations. It is quite possible in New York to lease an apartment on the thirty-fourth floor with a splendid and uninterrupted view and a great deal of sunlight only to find before a year has passed that both view and sunlight have been blocked out by a taller neighbour. It is even possible to live on a short, narrow street which suddenly, through an aldermanic whim, becomes longer and broader. Elevated and street-car lines, traditional for a quarter of a century or longer, have been known to disappear in a week.

Even a New York taxi-driver — and New York taxi-

drivers are celebrated for their charm, wit, and intelligence
— cannot hope to keep himself informed in regard to the
hotels, theatres, and restaurants. In Victorian days such
landmarks as Delmonico's and Martin's moved northward
every decade, the Harrigan Theatre became the Mansfield,
and later the Garrick. Now, the changes are accomplished
more swiftly. Almost before the last stone had been removed from the old Waldorf-Astoria, a new Waldorf-
Astoria was rising on Park Avenue. Stanford White's
Madison Square Garden, with its celebrated replica of the
Giralda Tower, *in Madison Square,* has been supplanted
by a Madison Square Garden on Eighth Avenue. Maxfield
Parrish's mural decoration representing Old King Cole
which so recently graced the Knickerbocker Hotel bar has
been transferred to the Racket Club, but what has become
of Saint-Gaudens's Diana nobody seems to know. Famous
old theatres devoted to the drama become moving picture
houses over night, and new theatres arise on every corner.
Only exceptionally does a hotel hold its prestige or its clientele over a long period, and when a friend telephones that
he is stopping at the New Neptune, although one has
never heard of it before, he knows that it is the latest thing
in hostelries. You must ask its location so that you can inform your taxi-driver, for he probably will not be acquainted with it. Probably even the telephone company
is ignorant of the telephone number and by the time it
learns it, the number will have been changed. Once Bryant,

Gramercy, Riverside, Columbus, Stuyvesant, Chelsea, and a few other simple names, suggestive of New York families and localities, designated the exchanges. Now scarcely a day passes but what some fantastic appellation like Lifeguard, Volunteer, Caledonia, Eldorado, Medallion, Galsworthy, or Nightingale is added to the list. It is not beyond possibility that there are more telephones in New York than there are people.

Like the restaurants — and many speakeasies *are* restaurants — this or that speakeasy or bootlegger goes in or out of fashion. It is one man's gin this month, another's next. A bootlegger must have unusual qualities to retain his custom over a long period of time. It is not that New Yorkers are more fickle than the citizens of another town, it is perhaps that they do not exist homogeneously. If they applaud this concert artist in 1927, and neglect him in 1928, if they buy their Corton 1915 on Sixth Avenue in 1929 and on Lexington Avenue in 1930, it is not so much because they are forgetful as because for the most part they are entirely different people who have moved in from London and Chicago while the New Yorkers of the twelve months' earlier period have gone to Africa, Palm Beach, and China. It is also quite certain, as Paul Morand has sapiently pointed out, that what is *new* in New York is always more beautiful and better than what is old. This statement may not be comprehensible to the inhabitants of Bruges or Segovia, but nevertheless it is quite true.

✳ PARTIES ✳

The noises and smells of New York are by comparison more constant. It is almost impossible at any season of the year or in any quarter of the city to escape the sound of blasting, which reminds one that Manhattan, like the Church of Rome, is built on solid rock, or the sound of riveting, that process by which molten bolts are urged to bind steel girders together. Sometimes these sounds are imminent and ear-splitting, sometimes they are dull rackets in the distance, but their permanence seems fairly secure. So does that of the rumble of the elevated railways, the clanging of bells on the trolley-cars, the shrieking of the taxi-sirens, the explosions of exhausted gas from automobiles, the late evening cries of Extra! (usually unheeded), proclaiming another edition of the tabloids, the song of the radio, Crying for the Carolines, through so many open windows or through the fragile floors or frail walls of apartment houses, the beating of the steam in cold radiators, Rudy Vallee and Duke Ellington, and in the morning, the hurling of tin trash-receptacles by the refuse man against brick walls or the clatter of milk-bottles upon cement floorings. These are a few of the predominant contemporary New York sounds, most of which did not exist twenty years ago and many of which may have departed in favour of newer dins in 1950.

The smells are more subtle. The faint odour of horse-dung, so prevailing in the nineties, has of course been supplanted by the aroma of gas. The other odours of New

❋ PARTIES ❋

York depend upon the locale and the seasons: in the summer, the smell of hot asphalt, a distinct smell of chop suey and occasionally even of cooking opium on Broadway and the adjacent streets; in the winter, the aroma of roasting chestnuts; in the theatres, the churches, and the restaurants the mingled odours of Guerlain, Houbigant, Hudnut, and stale tobacco.

The " sights " of New York change perpetually: McGowan's Pass Tavern, Jack's, Shanley's, Rectors, have all disappeared, while the new Casino in Central Park would not be on speaking terms with the old. The Brooklyn Bridge is still to be observed, but the Hudson Tube is a more modern wonder. Negro Harlem has supplanted Chinatown and the Bowery in the affections of those who seek diversion at night. The Woolworth Building, once the eighth wonder of the world, is no longer solitary or even paramount. Towers have sprung up on every hand — and continue to rise — until New York begins to resemble in the twilight a greater and more glittering San Gimignano in which the machine-gun battles of the gangsters and racketeers remind one of the mediæval conflicts between Guelphs and Ghibellines.

Occasionally it amused Hamish to do something out of the way, to behave in a manner that would be considered almost bad form by some of his friends. Thus, on a day in January, he happened into one of the large concert halls to

hear an English novelist give his views on modern literature. The hall was crowded when he entered, and he was
amazed when he took his seat to discover Noma Ridge occupying the next chair. She smiled, dimpling prettily, and
grasped his hand with some fervour.

It's such fun to astonish you, she said. You are astonished, aren't you?

I am, Hamish readily admitted.

I'm not going to try to confuse you, she went on. I came
here today to see somebody.

Not me? Hamish demanded in some alarm.

Of course not, silly. She smiled and squeezed his hand
again.

At this juncture the lecturer appeared on the platform.
He was tall and thin with a leonine head of hair, and one
of his eyes drooped lower than the other, giving his face a
perpetual quizzical expression. As he cleared his throat in
preparation for his lecture, the audience applauded vocif-
erously, and a plump lady sitting near Hamish actually
cheered.

The opening paragraphs of the lecture were extremely
dull and as the fellow went on sententiously draping plati-
tudes along the walls and over the chandeliers, Hamish
began to wonder why it was that English authors became
such great favourites on the platform in America. . . .
The romantic movement . . . Mr. Aldous Huxley, a
scientific scion of a scientific sire . . . the romantic

movement . . . Mr. Galsworthy's clarity . . . Not
much to be expected of Americans, I'm afraid . . . Mr.
Wells's eagerness . . . the barrenness and sterility of the
younger generation, especially in America . . . Miss
Rebecca West's witty explosions . . . Mr. Julian Green's
important contribution . . . after all there was the romantic movement. Life was getting better and better
and the art that reflected the cheering fact that this was
the best of all possible worlds was the best art. . .
At this point Hamish got up, very bored, nodded a
casual goodbye to Noma Ridge, yawned, and walked
out.

The sun was shining brightly. It was warm, but not too
warm: an ideal New York winter day. Hamish invariably
felt lost in the absence of David. What could he do? Buy
a camellia and ride in the Park? Shop in search of porce-
lain — Ginori, Rockingham, Lowestoft, or Copenhagen
— of which he was always enamoured, but for which at
present he had no very searching need? Call on his sister
whom he had not seen for several months? He could walk
up Madison Avenue or visit a speakeasy or a club where
he might encounter all the people he did not wish to meet
today, or he might go home to read a book: Bijou de Cein-
ture, a fascinating account of the training of boys for the
Chinese stage, or Natalie Barney's Aventures de l'Esprit,
or . . . He definitely decided that he did not wish to
telephone Rosalie Keith.

A little later, passing a drug-store, he dropped in, picked his way past popular novels, sandwiches, bicycles, cut-flowers, and men's bathing-suits, to enter a booth and call her number.

Hello, Rosalie.

Oh, it's you, Hamish. Don't you want to come up for a whisky and soda?

I don't think so. . . Hamish was yawning. . . I just called up to find out how you were.

Have you heard from David?

Oh, a coupla cablegrams and radios. You must have received some too.

Dozens. Full of strange threats against Siegfried, and very, very rude. Oh, Hamish, does David hate me?

I don't know, Rosalie. It's hard to tell what David likes and dislikes.

I know. Rilda has been so beastly. She hasn't been to dinner here since he left and she used to come practically every night. I didn't want her, of course, she went on reflectively, I never invited her. *Never.*

Oh, well, Rilda. Hamish yawned petulantly again. What do you think Noma Ridge would be doing at a lecture? he demanded with more interest.

Noma Ridge at a lecture! Are you *sure?* I never heard of such a thing. Was it a lecture on biology?

Certainly, I'm sure. She sat next to me. And it wasn't a lecture on biology.

You *too*. Well, perhaps that's the reason.

She couldn't have known I was going. I bought a ticket at the last possible moment. Besides, she didn't leave with me.

What was the lecture about?

I dunno. Mr. Galsworthy. . . The romantic movement. Best of . . .

I understand better now. Noma would go to hear about anything romantic.

Hamish yawned again. Why had he called this woman up? Goodbye, he said lamely and without prelude.

Wait a minute, Hamish! Won't you come to dinner tonight? Atalissa Carnforth will be there.

Well, you won't have to have any dinner if she comes. She always carries her own dinner in a little dressing-case, packed with thermos bottles and containers. She props the case in front of her and partakes. She refuses to eat other people's food.

All the more reason why *you* should come. There will be plenty in that case.

Well, perhaps. . . Hamish was more than dubious. . . You dine at eight-thirty, don't you?

Yes. Please try to come.

Goodbye, he said again.

Hamish hung up the receiver and yawned for the fifth time that afternoon. Why did he behave so perversely? He had cherished no desire to telephone Rosalie. It must have been some curious subconscious connection with his feeling about David that had impelled him to do it. He missed David frightfully. What could be keeping him in Europe? Why had he gone away at all? His drink-inspired cables only served to make Hamish feel more lonesome and unsettled. Hamish had sent a few drink-inspired cables himself. As a matter of fact he would have sailed to join David at once, could he be certain that David would wait for him. David's actions were unpredictable: he might even now be on the ocean, homeward bound. And Rilda? Poor Rilda. If David did not return presently something would have to be done about Rilda.

Glancing in a shop-window, Hamish observed a poster advertising a dance recital by Malvina Crane, " fresh from her European triumphs," and then he examined the street sign and noted that he was standing only a few doors from Donald's place and, unknown to himself, must have been heading there all the time. Try as he might, it seemed impossible for him to stay away for long from those who reminded him of David.

It was now four-thirty and Donald himself opened the door. Freddie was waiting on the customers and the front parlour was occupied by King Swan — Hamish was beginning to wonder if this man ever really drove a car — and, at another table, the Gräfin von Pulmernl und Stilzernl sitting with Roy Fern. His clothes were smartly cut and his hair pomaded with bear's grease until it shone like

the silver tip of the Chrysler Tower. His face was even
paler and his finger-nails longer and more pointed than
ever. Beaming with delight on her protégé, the Gräfin
shook her finger playfully at Hamish.

I'm delighted you've come, she exclaimed. Won't you
join us for a drink?

Hamish exchanged greetings with King Swan, shook
hands with Roy and the Gräfin and seated himself at their
table. Dead sober as he happened to be, he made an ap-
praisal of this curious and kind witch who sat beside him.
Her vitality was enormous, a bright flame that flared up
inside her wrinkled but not unsightly substance. It was
obvious that she had assumed complete charge of this boy
— the bootlegger's apprentice — but it was also obvious
that she demanded nothing of him in return. Rather, she
seemed to derive energy through parting with it. It was
quite likely that she retained sufficient vigour to master the
newest Harlem dance, but it was absolutely certain that in
return for what she did for him Roy Fern's hardest task
was to escort her to the speakeasies and night-clubs where
he would prefer to spend his time under any circumstances.

Hamish had ordered an old-fashioned whisky cocktail
which presently was borne to him by Donald himself who
now sank into a chair between King Swan and the trio.

Well, Roy has certainly hit it rich, he began, with that
disarming frankness which never annoyed anybody. Even
the hair-dresser visits him now, and probably even the

snow-vendors. I don't think he ever goes out except to take Adele.

At the mention of her Christian name, the Gräfin's face burst into a million-wrinkled smile. It amused the old lady mightily to hear a bootlegger, a chauffeur, or a Negro tap-dancer address her in a fashion which she would certainly not have permitted any nobleman in Germany to do.

I love the way Donald says Adele, she confessed. It's so much better than the German way!

Oh, hang me for a cow-thief and butter my asparagus! cried Donald who was always embarrassed by compliments.

In answer to the bell, Freddie unbolted the door to let Simone Fly enter.

Hello everybody, she cried, pulling off her hat and running her hand swiftly through her tousled hair. Her slenderness was clad in a black and grey checked tweed, with a blue satin blouse.

Has any one seen Beauty? she demanded.

Nobody's seen nobody, King Swan volunteered.

Why, hello, King. Whenever do you do any work?

Never you mind. Quit ridin' me. I drove Rilda to Harlem the other night, he added, knocking the ash from his cigar neatly into his trouser-cuff.

Rilda! When was that? Hamish asked quickly.

Oh, I dunno. We were up here and she was drunk and she wanted to go.

Did you bring her back? Hamish was white.

No, I didn't wait for her. She didn't ask me to wait.

She's all right, said Simone. I saw her yesterday. Rilda can get around by herself. She's got just as many legs and arms as I have. Rilda's all right. I'm glad you drove somebody somewhere, she assured King. It's the first time I ever heard of it.

Quit ridin' me, King Swan repeated sullenly.

Roy's pale, tortured face caught Hamish's attention. The boy was pulling at his coat-sleeve.

When's David coming back? Roy demanded feverishly.

Now that'll be about all for you, Donald said. Freddie, get the crowd something to drink.

Well, I want to know, Roy whimpered.

Nobody knows, said Hamish. Nobody except maybe Rilda or David . . .

He dunno, announced Donald, adding affectionately, *That* one!

We could go over and look for him, the Gräfin suggested. Roy's so unhappy without him. But I don't want to go back to Europe. I want to always stay in New York now . . . for ever and ever. We'll play around the speakeasies and Harlem till Coney Island opens and then I expect to take Roy down there to spend weeks. I've heard about a Half Moon Hotel and we'll go there and sleep and then make whoopee all day along the beach, digging for clams and dodging the roller coasters.

You aren't going to find Coney Island much after

Harlem, Simone Fly remarked. You shoulda started with Coney. Blaa! she shouted. Put some more gin in this, Freddie. . . . Simone planted her feet on top of the radio, exposing her long, slim legs, encased in ivory silk.

I want to see David, Roy continued to whimper. He's reg'lar.

Aw, shut up, you! Donald was losing his patience and his temper.

You shall too, if you want to, the Gräfin announced sympathetically. I'll send you over on the very next boat.

You will . . . sure? The boy's face proclaimed his vast delight.

I will. . . There were tears in the Gräfin's eyes.

But will David want to see *him?* Donald inquired with a touch of cynicism. Now, will he?

Hamish looked gloomily doubtful.

David'll be too drunk to recognize the kid, Simone remarked. Her jade cigarette-holder slipped through her fingers to splinter on the floor.

He'll want to see *me,* Roy protested.

We can ask him, suggested the Gräfin, but you've got to supply somebody else to go out with me, Donald.

I'll go out with you. I'd be glad to, King Swan responded. He stood up and bent double to tie his shoe, an act of which he was incapable while sitting.

The hell you will, cried Roy Fern angrily.

Now, now, easy, suggested Donald. Let the ants out of

your pants, Roy. You can't eat your caviar and have it too, you know. . . Then, to Adele: The place is full of people that'll be *de*-lighted to go out with you.

What's the matter with you anyway? Simone cried to Roy. Any one'd think you were better than King or worse or something. Blaaa! In her excitement, Simone dropped her glass and removed one foot from the radio to stretch it in the opposite direction on the carpet, so that she more or less resembled an extended compass.

David don't want him, Hamish said with great finality. He'd get over there only to find David on his way back.

I want to see David, the boy whiningly repeated.

You'll do as you're told, growled Donald. Quit the sob stuff.

I'll do what *you* tell me, of course, Donald, Roy, with brimming eyes, replied to his benefactor, only . . .

Who's going to Rosalie Keith's to dinner? Hamish interrupted him to demand.

I'm going to Harlem, the Gräfin announced firmly.

Not for dinner? Hamish inquired.

For the night, for the whole night, she went on gleefully. Fräulein Stupforsch has no idea where I am and I doubt if she ever discovers now.

Be yourself, Adele, Donald advised her gently.

I want to see David, whined Roy.

See here, you, cried Donald, turning on Roy savagely, I've had about enough of your blubber. Adele dresses you

152

up and feeds you and leads you to bales of snow and lakes of hard liquor and you want to look up somebody that don't know you're alive. Even if we cabled him he'd be too blind to answer. The chances are he's on his way back this minute. If he isn't it's none of your goddam business. You go to Harlem with Adele and like it.

I'm tired, the boy protested.

Blaaa! cried Simone Fly, waving her arms wildly about her head.

Tired, my left foot! Donald retorted. You're full of up-pies, that's what ails you. If you sneezed you'd sneeze your whole goddam guts out.

Don't tease him, Donald, the Gräfin implored. If Roy doesn't want to go with me, King says . . .

At your service, lady. The chauffeur rose and made an extremely successful bow.

No, *please!* screamed Roy. I won't have you go out with him.

You behave then, Donald adjured him roughly. Then, turning to Hamish, he whispered, I'll go to Rosalie's with you. I gotta take a case of champagne to her and if I do that she'll expect me to stay to dinner and lay her. Sure, I'll go with you. It won't be so bad if you come along, but I can't stay late. After dinner I gotta make a quick turn. I gotta go hear Walter Hampden play Richelieu.

❋ *ELEVEN* ❋

Hamish had been to a tea, as cocktail parties are still occasionally called in New York, for the great English novelist, attended by most of the local literati. The visiting celebrity talked a great deal about himself, his plots and plans, and the others talked a great deal about themselves, their plots and plans. Fortunately, nobody listened to anybody else. Hamish left this house to drift, by way of taxi, into another cocktail party given for a lady who had left society to become an actress by an actress who had given up the stage to become a lady. They both explained why at great length, although everybody had heard the story many times before. But that was quite all right because again nobody listened. With a Negro poet and Gareth Johns, the novelist, whom he encountered at this party, Hamish went on to an apartment in Harlem where the drinks were better and the guests more attractive-looking, but he was still restless and an hour or so later, he drove down through the Park and went to a fourth party in Gramercy Park where he ran into Noma Ridge.

Hello, Hamish, she accosted him, you must begin to believe that I'm pursuing you.

Well, aren't you? he inquired.

Not particularly. I don't mind telling you I think you're wonderful, I think you're swell.

There's music to that, Hamish retorted.

I know, Noma assented impatiently. Do stop talking nonsense. It's David I want.

Oh, that's your line, is it?

It's part of my line. Not the best part, perhaps. I'd like to tell you . . .

I'm sure you would. Everybody's been telling me all the afternoon. Why?

You know perfectly well why, but we can't talk here. Let's run over to Donald's.

Where it's more public.

That's what I mean. Nobody will listen to us here. It's a waste of time talking before these people.

At the Wishbone, however, it developed that Noma must have been speaking ironically, as she asked for a private room.

That's easy, Donald assured her. The private rooms are always empty. My customers are exhibitionists.

Ushered into a small green chamber, they seated themselves side by side on a couch, crossed their legs decorously, and Hamish proceeded to attack the drink that red-headed Freddie provided for him.

I've been awfully in love eight times, Noma began, and I've had consuming, flaming affairs with every one of the eight. Of course, she added complacently, I've slept with lots of people I wasn't in love with, lots and lots.

Men?

Mostly. Some boys and . . .

Yeah? Hamish inquired in a casual tone.

Well, not often. I don't like it much.

Did they?

They said so. I didn't ask you here to talk about *that*.

I suspected as much.

I want to talk about myself.

Who doesn't? Hamish demanded.

Love is like picnicking, Noma went on. It's all right when one is very young to eat one's lunch lying about on the damp grass, but later in life we are likely to be more comfortable at the Ritz. It's more convenient in the long run to substitute affection or passion for the grand emotion. Nevertheless, against my will, I've fallen in love with David, and I want to explain why. Nobody else, after all, can be as interesting about herself as I can, don't you think so, Hamish?

Hamish shook his head without much conviction.

When you think of me you think of a charnel-house of dead lovers, don't you?

I hadn't said so. I don't think of you often.

Now, Hamish, don't be beastly. You can be so incredibly nasty when you want to be. You do think of me as a charnel-house, don't you? she pleaded.

Well, perhaps a little bit like that, if you want me to, he responded wearily, draining his drink with a kind of fury. It did seem extremely difficult to get drunk today.

I knew you did, she cried triumphantly, and you're entirely wrong. I'm not a particle like that. It's merely that I'm so sensitive and sensible that I'm always searching and expect to find perfection. You can't find perfection without looking for it, trying a lot of things that fall short of it, can you? she demanded.

He shook his head slowly.

There, you see! I knew you would understand, she exclaimed. If, for example, you were in a strange city and wanted to find a perfect restaurant, you wouldn't be satisfied with the first one you walked into, would you?

I suppose not.

You would eat here and there, all over the place, until you were certain you had discovered what you were looking for, wouldn't you?

I suppose so, Hamish admitted yawning.

Well, that is what I have done with men. . .

And . . .

Not so often. That is what I have done with men, she repeated, and I have made what I consider a great discovery. The men I was not in love with have been more satisfactory in bed than the men I loved.

Then why do you want David? You say you are in love with David.

I know. It sounds silly to you. . . She hesitated before she explained, I'm sure David will prove to be the exception.

I don't possibly see how you can be sure of that.

I *am* sure of it. I have my intuitions, you know. There would be no meaning to my experiences if they had not taught me to have my intuitions. I have my pride too. I don't like people to lie about me. I tell the truth about myself, you know. Why shouldn't other people tell the truth about me.

I'll say you do. Why in hell did you want to tell it to me?

Hamish, you've got to quit being such a bloody swine. You know perfectly well why I want to talk to you. I want you to help me with David.

As Freddie opened the door at this moment to bring another drink, a sepulchral voice could be heard announcing: Madame Povla Frijsh, whom you have just heard sing Von ewiger Liebe by Brahms, is a queenly woman. I wish you could see her. She is wearing a taffeta dress draped with black lace, very décolleté . . . The door closed again.

Hamish threw back his head and laughed. In the first place, young lady, he replied, I don't even know where David is.

That's unimportant. Soon or late, he'll turn up and that's when I want your help.

It won't do you any good. David loves Rilda.

Perhaps, but he sleeps with everybody else.

Hamish qualified this statement: He hates everybody else.

❊ PARTIES ❊

After he has enjoyed them. I don't care what David thinks of me or what he says about me. I think I'd love to be insulted by David. Anyway, I must have him . . .

His back propped against the wall, Hamish meditated while Noma talked on. What was the attraction that David exerted to such a marked degree? Why did everybody who knew him talk and think so much about him? Questioning himself thus, for an instant Hamish hated David, hated him bitterly, actually wished him dead, but presently his habitual warm affection swept away this strange mood of disloyalty. A wave of softness, a melting mood of deep love for David possessed him and answered his question. Hamish *knew* why every one was attracted towards David. Who was more attracted than himself?

And where was David, David who continually tried to escape from these demonstrations of passion, to escape from Rilda even, to escape from himself most of all? Where was David? In a vision, as Noma Ridge went on endlessly talking about herself, her desires, and her tastes, Hamish, un-listening, saw David in the arms of some woman. Irene, perhaps: the thought stabbed him, but he realized that he would give David anything he required. The worst of it is, Hamish reflected, that David requires nothing. He only yields now and then to the requirements of others.

Why, Hamish, I don't believe you're listening at all, he heard Noma say.

Of course I'm listening, he growled.

Then, why don't you answer my questions?

They're too silly to be answered.

Noma rose with some dignity.

Really, Hamish, you are impossible, she said. Please take me out of this dive.

As they passed through the corridor Hamish was startled to catch a glimpse of Irma Oberhalter — what could she be doing in the Wishbone? — while the voice over the radio announced: Madame Povla Frijsh is a Spanish woman and this is her début on the air. She is one of the greatest singers of the world and you all must know that she is a Danish woman.

Freddie opened the door to let them out, and Hamish hoped his interview with Noma was over. It proved to be: their departure was interrupted by a familiar figure, Rilda, unsteadily mounting to Donald's apartment, Rilda with dishevelled hair, blood-shot eyes, and a haggard countenance that bore evidence of recent weeping, a sorry and bedraggled Rilda.

When she saw the couple on the steps above her, she stopped and confronted them sullenly.

As Hamish, believing her about to fall, rushed to her assistance she received the proffered shelter of his arms, pleading, Oh, God, Hamish, where is David? I can't live another day without David!

✳ *TWELVE* ✳

To an extremely indignant Noma, Hamish bade a curt farewell, and turning his attention to Rilda, half-dragged, half-carried her downstairs. She clung to him in a kind of pathetic despair and when he had seated her in a taxi apparently she fell asleep against his shoulder. Quite suddenly he felt a very strong impulse. Kissing the unresponsive lips of the unconscious Rilda, he whispered, I love you, again and again.

She did not reply. She made no movement of any kind. After a time he stopped kissing her. When, however, the taxi halted before her door and he shook her to awaken her, she rose so readily that it scarcely seemed possible that she had actually been asleep.

Come in, Hamish, she urged him, and put me to bed.

With his assistance, she managed to make her way through the hallway into the elevator and before her apartment door she huskily instructed him how he might discover her key in her bag. Once inside, she pressed the button which flooded the drawing-room with light, and shed her fur cloak. To his astonishment Hamish learned that she was clad only in a chiffon night-dress of sea-shell pink.

Huddled in one corner of a great couch she muttered

thickly: I was lonely, Hamish, terribly lonely. I just couldn't bear it any more. Didn't want to send for Siegfried. Just wanted to go out. Don't know what I wanted. . . . She began to cry softly again.

Seating himself beside her, Hamish drew her head to his shoulder.

Why, dearest Rilda, he demanded, didn't you send for me?

I thought . . . You haven't been near me, Hamish. Thought you didn't want to come.

My God, Rilda, Siegfried . . .

Siegfried! Her tone was so scornful that he scanned her face closely for a clue, but she had closed her eyes and her expression was placid.

Do you want me to stay? he inquired presently.

She opened her eyes and looked up into his. Course I want you to stay, want you to stay, want you to stay, she mumbled. I'll hate you 'fyou do, but I'll hate you more 'fyou don't.

I'm afraid I should hate myself if I did, Hamish said. You see, David . . .

Oh, David! Rilda, rousing herself, cried in fury. Everybody always thinks about David. What would David want? A lot he thinks about *us!* The swine. The beastly, filthy swine!

He . . .

I know what you're going to say. I'll say it myself: why

shouldn't he go away and leave me? When he's in New York with me it's worse. We are destroying each other, Hamish, eating each other alive. . . Want to forget him, trying hard to forget him, he's trying to forget me . . . can't, can't, can't. . . She clenched her fists. . . Stay with me tonight, Hamish, so I'll have some good reason for hating somebody besides myself. Stay with me while I call out *his* name.

She buried her face in his breast and sobbed convulsively. Hamish stroked her head softly, attempting to soothe her, and quite suddenly and unexpectedly, she fell asleep. He carried her very gently into her bedroom, and placed her on the bed, covering her with a satin dressing-gown. Returning to the drawing-room, he telephoned Donald to discover where the Gräfin might be. She had, it appeared, just arrived at the Wishbone and when apprised, over the telephone, of the situation, she agreed to come over at once, if she might bring Roy with her. Hamish, exhausted, left the telephone to extend himself full-length on the couch. Mopping his perspiring face with his handkerchief, he realized what a narrow escape he had had. Every one forgave David anything, but no one would have forgiven him, Hamish. Least of all, David. . . No . . . least of all, Rilda. Well, she had helped him, helped him by professing what everybody seemed to feel, her greater love for David. What was there about David that made people love him so much? Hamish, pondering, suspected that the greater part of the secret was David's rich indifference as to whether they did or not.

His desire for, and actual need of, a drink was so imperative that he forced himself to sit up, and presently dragged himself to a standing posture. He was so completely exhausted that he almost staggered as he made his way through the dining-room into the bar where he poured out a stiff pony of brandy and gulped it down. He found it advisable to repeat this prescription for the alleviation of fatigue, before he returned to the drawing-room with his energy somewhat restored.

It had been some time since he had visited Rilda, but a casual inspection of the room did not indicate changes. The walls were panelled in an ivory-white satin damask and the furniture was upholstered in the same material. On a bargueño rose a lamp in the form of a Chinese nun, cut from coral, on a malachite base. A figure of a tortoise fashioned from turquoise occupied a table, while on the piano stood an amber bowl filled with Talisman roses with their petals of yellow, rose, and copper. The carpet, too, was ivory-white, and the walls were quite destitute of pictures. The room preserved its accustomed simplicity and a certain frigidity. There seemed to be no changes and yet Hamish was aware of some subtle departure from normality. Seeking to discover the nature of this difference, he made a more minute inspection of the room and was rewarded eventually when he found a silver sword which, upon examination, bore the name of Siegfried engraved on the hilt. Hamish sat down to muse, with the sword across his knee. Rilda did not awaken and how long he sat half-dozing before the ringing bell aroused him, he could not be sure.

When he opened the door, the Gräfin, warmly wrapped in sables, entered, closely followed by Roy Fern in a shaggy bear-skin coat. Roy was a trifle paler than usual and seemed more slender, once the coat was removed.

Where is Rilda? the Gräfin demanded in a stage whisper.

She's asleep, Hamish replied, in his ordinary tone. I don't think we can wake her.

The Gräfin turned to her escort. Run along into the bar and find yourself a drink, she adjured him. I'm sure Rilda won't mind. But, please, Roy, keep off the uppies tonight.

The Gräfin removed her cloak and seated herself in a white fauteuil, her feet as usual swinging a little clear of the floor. She seemed younger than usual and more energetic, Hamish thought.

Now, what is this? she demanded, looking him very squarely in the eyes.

From the bar came the cheerful sound of clinking glasses and opening bottles.

Hamish tried very hard to avoid the honest and stead-fast gaze of this extraordinary and kind old lady's face, framed under her bonnet, but he found it impossible to do so entirely. It was, however, with half-averted eyes that he replied, Rilda was afraid to be alone. I thought perhaps you could stay here tonight with her.

I could stay here tonight — and Roy, too, if there is enough for him to drink — she announced, but her tone was less than hearty, and it appeared to Hamish that she had the manner of a person who could not believe the evidence of her ears.

I hate to have you misunderstand, he said and then repeated with altered emphasis, I hate to have *you* misunderstand.

There, there, dear boy . . . she restored a more affectionate note to her voice . . . the things you do and say in America are sometimes a little puzzling to a funny, old lady brought up in Central Europe, but you have made me very happy here, you Americans, and I will not complain. Do and say what you like. Be as odd as you please and I will try to understand. After all the ways of two races are different. Only, in my country no man who felt the way you do about Rilda — and her husband away too — would call up an old lady from Central Europe to take his place. However, I dare say you know what you are doing and anyway I'd do anything for you and Rilda even if you didn't know what you were doing or what you wanted done.

The Gräfin tiptoed to Rilda's door, listened outside for a moment, then turned the handle softly and entered.

Emerging, she closed the door, and returning to the drawing-room, assured Hamish: She's all right, sleeping soundly. You can go now. I'll lie down in David's room and put Roy on the couch here. Where is that boy?

But I thought I'd stay here too, Hamish explained.

You thought you'd stay here too!

Yes.

But where will you sleep?

I probably won't sleep at all, he said. I'll just lie about in a chair.

So I am here in the capacity of chaperon, the old lady chuckled. What a country! What a country! I'm sure David would never behave like this, but I like you anyway, Hamish, no matter how you behave. . . Turning her head, she called, Roy, where are you?

Presently the reply came back: Here I am, Adele, and the boy, his eyes gleaming unnaturally, his trembling hand clutching a tumblerful of gin, appeared in the doorway.

Her glance was severe. Roy, she demanded, you haven't been taking any uppies?

No, Adele.

I believe you. Roy, we're going to spend the night here. I shall sleep in David's bed, and you can sleep on the couch unless you want to go back to the bar and get drunker.

Yes, Adele.

What a delightful boy! she remarked to Hamish with

some pride. As soon as we find out where David is, I shall ship him over at once.

But David won't want him, Hamish protested.

Nonsense, pronounced the old lady with complete finality. David always gives people what they want. He wouldn't make anybody unhappy if he could help it.

He's making Rilda damned unhappy, Hamish cried, and he's making me . . .

You're making him unhappy, you mean, the Gräfin retorted with sombre dignity. The trouble with you and Rilda is that neither of you knows what you want of David. If you knew, and he could do so, David would give it to you. That's David's charm, in giving freely what is demanded of him.

At this point, Roy Fern, who had been standing in the doorway listening intently, allowed his glass of gin to slip through his fingers, flung himself on his belly, and began to weep violently.

Kneeling beside him, the Gräfin tried to comfort him.

My dear, dear boy, she repeated again and again, as she softly stroked his head.

Eventually, she succeeded in coaxing him to assume a sitting posture and a little later, with some aid from Hamish, she managed to lead him to the couch, where she loosened his collar while Hamish unlaced his shoes and removed them.

It's a shame, she assured him, that David doesn't know

how unhappy you are. If David knew, he would send for you.

When, somewhat later, Roy fell asleep, the Gräfin bade Hamish goodnight and retired to David's bedroom. Hamish fetched the bottle of brandy from the bar and settling himself in an arm-chair, prepared to await the dawn.

❋ THIRTEEN ❋

In midwinter in New York Mei-Lan-Fang introduced his traditional Oriental art to large groups of delighted Occidentals; ten thousand fish, including an eel four feet long, were removed from the Central Park reservoir; Babe Ruth signed a contract with Col. Ruppert to play ball with the Yankees for two more years at a salary of $160,000; the Europa came into port with an ocean record; Webster Hall, on East Eleventh Street, the scene of so many radical balls, burned down; Mrs. Patrick Campbell lectured on Beautiful Speech and the Art of Acting; Anthony Mortelito stabbed the head keeper at Auburn Prison seven times with a crude, improvised knife; William Howard Taft died; La Argentinita presented the authentic beauty of Spanish dancing to an unappreciative Broadway audience; Charles Schwab's historic Riverside Drive château was sold to an apartment-house builder; the Havemeyer collection of paintings and art objects was opened to the public at the Metropolitan Museum; four thousand persons, trying to get into the Natural History Museum to see a showing of a film developing the Einstein theory of relativity, overturned cases, broke windows and doors, and injured one another; a " modernistic " Childs restaurant was opened on Lexington Avenue; Maurice Chevalier sang

※ *PARTIES* ※

Dites-moi, ma mère; the news-reel at the Embassy, a moving picture theatre, informed the public pictorially that Sydney Franklin, a Brooklyn boy turned matador, had been gored by a savage bull in the Plaza de Toros at Madrid; the planet Pluto was discovered; Toscanini conducted the Philharmonic Society in the Bacchanale from Tannhäuser, the Ride of the Valkyries, and the Trauermarsch from Götterdämmerung (this last in commemoration of the death of Frau Cosima Wagner) in so superb a manner that hoary-headed music lovers searched their memories in vain for comparisons; Marc Connelly gave God back to the world in The Green Pastures; forty thousand communists, gathered peaceably in Union Square, were trampled down in cossack fashion by the horses of the mounted police, while children were knocked over the heads with clubs; a jury of twelve men was unable to agree concerning the pornographic aspects of a play entitled The Pleasure Man by the ebullient Mae West and as a consequence the defendant regained her precarious liberty; and in an Italian restaurant on Macdougal Street ten canaries, accompanying a performance over the radio, sang in lusty unison the Overture to William Tell and negotiated the high notes in the sextet from Lucia.

The social life of the metropolis also continued. In mid-winter in New York, as in other capitals of the world, a great many dinner-, theatre-, and luncheon-parties were given. Guests were invited to formal and informal dances and to observe prize-fighting, wrestling, dance marathons, and six-day bicycle races. There were musical entertainments and extended yachting parties which embraced cruises to the West Indies or even to the Pacific, by way of the Canal and the glamour of Panama City. In these respects, perhaps, New York life did not differ to any great extent from that of other great cities during the season, but in another respect, the matter of cocktail parties, since the laws were passed prohibiting the sale of liquor, it could be said that more were held in one day in Manhattan than in a month elsewhere. A man with an extensive acquaintance, therefore, could drink steadily in New York from the beginning of cocktail time until eleven in the evening without any more expense than that entailed by car- or cab-fare.

The Gräfin, occasionally, as a matter of pride, perhaps, made a valiant effort to take in as many cocktail parties as possible, but she was somewhat handicapped by the behaviour of Roy Fern who was likely to get so very drunk at the first house he visited — or even before, at Donald Bliss's — that it was difficult to get him to move on. Frequently, indeed, it was necessary for some one to carry him in and out of the waiting automobile in which he was swiftly borne from one cocktail shaker to another. Nevertheless, when he sensed the fact that there was more liquor to be drunk, he made a brave effort, often successful, to revive sufficiently to do more than his share in getting rid of it. Curiously enough, Roy became more sober, at least in effect, as the evening proceeded, and by one in the morning often was able to walk in an almost stately manner.

To the Gräfin he was an infinite source of comfort and satisfaction. He was adequately vicious to stand apart from the rest of the world without being aggressive or disagreeable, save on rare occasions. Picturesque in appearance, he was very little more bother than a Pekinese. He appealed, indeed, to the mother instinct in the Gräfin much as a dog would do. To Roy, the Gräfin was like some incomprehensible goddess of infinite providence who had suddenly descended from heaven or Central Europe to bestow unlimited dozens of quarts of gin upon him, not to mention the wherewithal to purchase now and then — in strange toilet-rooms and in minor drug-stores, behind illicit counters piled high with Grosset and Dunlap books and ham-sandwiches — packets of that efficacious white powder known affectionately as snow, although this was done without her sanction, indeed against her expressed desire. She also promised now and again that she would lure David back or send Roy to David, and doubtless might have done so, no matter how much pain such a parting would have caused her, had there come to her any inkling of David's whereabouts. It was amazing that in return for her bounty she demanded no more than companionship.

One day in late winter which was so heavenly bright

that all New York with one accord pulled down the shades, illuminated its rooms with artificial light, and manufactured synthetic gin in a thousand bathtubs, the pair turned up at Rosalie Keith's.

I want to introduce you to Mrs. Alonzo W. Syreno, Rosalie was saying to the Gräfin, who had finally hesitated before the log fire in the library on the second floor. Mrs. Syreno is a friend of our David.

I am charmed to meet your Highness, Mrs. Syreno said, dropping a curtsy she had learned from a friend who had been presented at the Court of St. James's.

And where is our David? the Gräfin inquired politely and a little sadly. She realized that as long as she did not know the answer to this question she might keep Roy by her side.

Where's David? Roy echoed, almost fiercely.

Mrs. Alonzo W. Syreno never missed an opportunity to look at any male, however insignificant, but one glance at Roy was sufficient to cause her to give her complete attention to the Gräfin.

I don't know, she replied. I met him on the boat going over and then I saw him in London. I knew him very well, but, you could scarcely say intimately. . . Mrs. Syreno smiled enigmatically and accepted a cocktail from a tray a waiter was passing. . . You see, I went to Paris to get a divorce. Mr. Alonzo W. Syreno is as good as gold, but I got bored with him. Besides, he treated me badly, locked

me up in the preserve-closet. If it hadn't been for the milkman . . .

What was the milkman doing in the preserve-closet?
the Gräfin demanded.

But Mr. Syreno came to Paris too, ahead of me, Mrs.
Syreno continued, ignoring the Gräfin's query, and when
I arrived he was keeping company with a mouse-like creature, a dove-like creature. You know . . . Mrs. Syreno
pursed her lips and made a wry face.

The Gräfin nodded and Mrs. Alonzo W. Syreno
smirked and went on: I wouldn't have it. I just wouldn't
have it. I decided to let Miss Hortense Caldwell have
the game, while I kept the name. It's a pretty *name,*
isn't it?

Yes, indeed, the Gräfin replied, while Roy at her side
was forcing his long nails into the palms of his hands, and
David?

Oh yes, David . . . Where was I? Well, your Highness, I met Mr. Alonzo W. Syreno by appointment arranged by our lawyers, and I told him I was coming back
to New York to take up my rightful place in Knickerbocker
society — the Syrenos are a very old family, your Highness — and he was willing enough to give me the money,
all I wanted in fact, so that he could go to St. Moritz with
the lady mouse and so . . .

Is David in Paris? Roy's thirst for information in this
regard was pathetic.

❋ PARTIES ❋

Oh, David this and David that! You ask a lot about David here, Mrs. Alonzo W. Syreno remarked petulantly.

Rilda, surprisingly, joined the group, Rilda looking particularly attractive in a grey-blue riding habit, and carrying a crop. She was accompanied by Siegfried.

Her face was harassed, her eyes proclaimed her torture, as she began: I hear you've seen David.

Mrs. Alonzo W. Syreno opened her eyes very wide. And you are?

Mrs. Westlake.

Did you find out about David? Rosalie Keith demanded of the group.

I think, said Claire Madrilena, who heard this remark in passing, that the beautiful Mrs. Syreno must have our David concealed somewhere.

Did I hear the name of David? Hamish demanded from the doorway.

She won't tell a goddam thing and she knows, Roy Fern asserted fiercely, helping himself to another cocktail.

Mrs. Alonzo W. Syreno smiled deprecatingly. I never would have imagined, she remarked with an icy distinctness, that any man could possibly arouse so much interest in so many people. Mr. Alonzo W. Syreno has only been fortunate enough to interest two, one of them very slightly.

The woman is maddening, cried Rilda, maddening!

At least, Rosalie reminded her, she was invited to my house.

Steady, Rosalie, Siegfried adjured her. Rilda came with me.

What's up about David? inquired Simone Fly casually, sauntering up, cocktail in hand.

I think you all must be crazy, Mrs. Alonzo W. Syreno cried, quite crazy. If I knew anything about David I wouldn't tell you. He wouldn't want me to, was her added inspiration.

Roy Fern emitted a growl of rage at this.

David is my friend, he protested.

He's everybody's friend, was Rilda's emendation.

My dear . . . The Gräfin offered Rilda her sympathy and her hand while Siegfried silently pressed her other hand.

There was a moment's lull, as the butler passed another tray of cocktails. Without disengaging Siegfried's hand, Noma Ridge took advantage of the opportunity to ask him to call on her, an invitation which he accepted.

Did you all know, Rosalie demanded unexpectedly, that Buddy Parsons and Malvina Crane were married this afternoon?

Buddy! Hamish groaned. And Kim Skene?

Oh, Kim! Blaa! Simone Fly replied in her gutteral voice, turning her chic, guttersnipe face upwards until it was nearly horizontal, Midnight Blue has got him now.

I'm tired, Rilda announced. Rosalie always has such foul cocktails. I can't think why I come here.

You know damned well why you come here, a now thoroughly exasperated Rosalie retorted, and it's not to see me.

Siegfried nudged Rilda. Come along, he suggested. Let's drop into some speakeasy or other.

Let's find a new one, Rilda cried wildly. I'm sick of Donald's. He's too beautiful and successful. It's going to his liquor.

In a corner of the room Mrs. Alonzo W. Syreno sat drinking with Hamish.

You sorta remind me of David, she explained. You two sorta have the same manner. I was the baby wife of Mr. Alonzo W. Syreno, she went on. He treated me very badly. Wouldn't give me any freedom. Locked me in the preserve-closet. I'd be there yet if it hadn't been for the milkman.

What, demanded an astonished Hamish, was the milkman doing in the preserve-closet?

Mrs. Syreno did not answer this question. She continued with her narrative: I knew positively nothing when I married that man. I went to Paris to divorce him, but he was running around with a field-mouse or a wren and I thought better of it. I shall see that their child is not born in wedlock.

Are you sure there'll be a child? Hamish inquired.

If Mrs. Syreno contemplated replying to this question she never achieved her intention. She was interrupted by

Simone Fly who thrust her over-powdered face into the doorway long enough to shout: Iturbi is the greatest pianist that ever lived, that ever lived, that ever lived! The greatest . . . !

Her voice rose to a shriek as she collapsed on the floor, a heap of blue and white crêpe from which her long legs protruded.

As Noma Ridge walked over her prostrate form, she remarked, to no one in particular: I don't care very much for piano playing, do you?

I don't hear any, replied Mrs. Alonzo W. Syreno.

Is the rumour true that you know David? Noma asked her.

My God, another one!

As great as Nijinsky! Simone feebly shouted from the floor. Give the little Spanish boy a hand, and give the little Fly girl a drink.

Certainly, Simone, replied Hamish. What do you want? Clover club, old-fashioned whisky, Martini, Manhattan, Bronx, alexander, bacardi, orange blossom, Columbus, or a woojums?

Mix 'em, suggested Simone, still on the floor. I'm moanin' low.

There's music to that, Hamish remarked, as he rescued an absinthe cocktail from the butler's tray and handed it to her.

I know, Noma said impatiently. Then, to Mrs. Alonzo

W. Syreno, she persisted: Is it true that you know David?

Yes, I know David, that one replied insolently. I'll tell the world I know David Westlake. What of it?

Can you tell me where he is? Noma's eyes and voice were insolent.

Yes, I can, but I won't, Mrs. Syreno snapped.

As two strange young men entered the room in the only way possible by stepping over Simone's recumbent figure, she muttered darkly, Just a coupla pansies. Gimme a drink.

Get up and get one. It'll do you good, Hamish suggested.

What'll do her good, getting up or the drink? one of the young men inquired.

There's a lot of actresses and racketeers and gangsters downstairs, Simone announced. Don't tell me. Blaaa! *I know*. If I could get down there I would be too.

We'll carry you down, suggested one of the two unknown young men, and the two lifted her, probably with excellent intentions, but it was evident presently that they had dropped her on the stairs, a fact announced to the room above by a thud and the hoarse croaks of Simone.

Now, the Gräfin, who had not been seen in the library for some time, returned, followed by Roy. Approaching Hamish she apprised him of current events: Rilda has fallen asleep on Rosalie's bed, and Rosalie has taken Siegfried off to the coal-cellar or somewhere where nobody will follow them. I want to get off to see the Lindy Hop, she went on.

It's too early, Adele, Hamish explained.

That's what I told her. Gimme a drink, Roy demanded imperiously of the butler.

I think not for the Lindy Hop. It is in a dance-hall, not a night-club, the Gräfin explained.

What is the Lindy Hop, your Highness? Mrs. Alonzo W. Syreno demanded.

Oh, something in the air done in Harlem without airplanes, Hamish replied.

They're black mostly and they kick their legs out. . . The effect of this remark of Roy Fern's on the crowd could not have been greater had they learned he had written a book on comparative religion.

Yes, that's it, Noma Ridge corroborated his succinct statement, they're black and they kick their legs out.

They do something bellywise, too, Roy admitted. Gimme a drink.

I must see it! I must see it! The Gräfin clapped her hands with anticipatory glee, and accepted another cocktail.

David would like the Lindy Hop. Where is David? Roy demanded of Mrs. Alonzo W. Syreno.

Oh, David! she replied contemptuously. I'm sick of your David.

What's that! Roy was ferocious at once. Damn you! he cried, and thrust his fist within an inch of her face.

Mrs. Alonzo W. Syreno screamed, as Hamish pulled the excited boy away from her.

It's the uppies, the Gräfin explained to Mrs. Syreno, sighing at the same time. I can't make him stop.

At this moment Rilda appeared in the doorway.

Let's get out of here, she cried, flicking her crop across her knee. Rosalie's being rotten. Let's go on to the Lindy Hop.

To the Lindy Hop! Noma echoed.

To the Lindy Hop! repeated the Gräfin. Then, her face breaking into one of her enchanting, wrinkled smiles, she added unctuously, And how!

❊ FOURTEEN ❊

Every decade or so some Negro creates or discovers or stumbles upon a new dance step which so completely strikes the fancy of his race that it spreads like water poured on blotting paper. Such dances are usually performed at first inside and outside of lowly cabins, on levees, or, in the big cities, on street-corners. Presently, quite automatically, they invade the more modest night-clubs where they are observed with interest by visiting entertainers who, sometimes with important modifications, carry them to a higher low world. This process may require a period of two years or longer for its development. At just about this point the director of a Broadway revue in rehearsal, a hoofer, or even a Negro who puts on " routines " in the big musical shows, deciding that the dance is ready for white consumption, introduces it, frequently with the announcement that he has invented it. Nearly all the dancing now to be seen in our musical shows is of Negro origin, but both critics and public are so ignorant of this fact that the production of a new Negro revue is an excuse for the revival of the hoary old lament that it is a pity the Negro can't create anything for himself, that he is obliged to imitate the white man's revues. This, in brief, has been the history of the Cake-Walk, the Bunny Hug, the Turkey

Trot, the Charleston, and the Black Bottom. It will probably be the history of the Lindy Hop.

The Lindy Hop made its first official appearance in Harlem at a Negro Dance Marathon staged at Manhattan Casino some time in 1928. Executed with brilliant virtuosity by a pair of competitors in this exhibition, it was considered at the time a little too difficult to stand much chance of achieving popular success. The dance grew rapidly in favour, however, until a year later it was possible to observe an entire ball-room filled with couples devoting themselves to its celebration.

The Lindy Hop consists in a certain dislocation of the rhythm of the fox-trot, followed by leaps and quivers, hops and jumps, eccentric flinging about of arms and legs, and contortions of the torso only fittingly to be described by the word epileptic. After the fundamental steps of the dance have been published, the performers may consider themselves at liberty to improvise, embroidering the traditional measures with startling variations, as a coloratura singer of the early nineteenth century would endow the score of a Bellini opera with roulades, runs, and shakes.

To observe the Lindy Hop being performed at first induces gooseflesh, and second, intense excitement, akin to religious mania, for the dance is not of sexual derivation, nor does it incline its hierophants towards pleasures of the flesh. Rather it is the celebration of a rite in which glorification of self plays the principal part, a kind of terpsichorean megalomania. It is danced, to be sure, by couples, but the individuals who compose these couples barely touch each other during its performance, and each may dance alone, if he feels the urge. It is Dionysian, if you like, a dance to do honour to wine-drinking, but it is not erotic. Of all the dances yet originated by the American Negro, this the most nearly approaches the sensation of religious ecstasy. It could be danced, quite reasonably and without alteration of tempo, to many passages in the Sacre de Printemps of Stravinsky, and the Lindy Hop would be as appropriate for the music, which depicts in tone the representation of certain pagan rites, as the music would be appropriate for the Lindy Hop.

The Gräfin, after ascending a long flight of marble stairs, gasped her astonishment as she entered the great hall with its ample dance-floor enclosed on three sides by a brass railing behind which tables and chairs were provided for spectators and those who desired light refreshment. The fourth side of the floor was occupied by a long platform on which sat two bands of musicians which alternated in providing stimulation for the feet of the dancers. The floor at the moment was filled with Negroes, dancing as the Gräfin felt everybody should dance. She had frequently before watched Negro dancing with delight, but all the dancing she had hitherto seen was professional, or sexual, or merely the casual expression of a lazy rhythm.

This dancing was exalted, uplifting, dangerously exciting to the mere observer. It was evident that the performers felt its spirit even more keenly. The band, too, had fallen under the magic spell, playing a wild tune, in which saxophones, drums, and banjos vied one with the other to create new effects in rhythm, in harmony, or in the decoration of the melody.

Leaning a little on King Swan and Roy, the Gräfin pressed forward to the ringside table that had been reserved for her, and presently she pushed aside a proffered beverage to devote her attention to the miracle of movement spread before her. She was, she was fully aware, not sitting in a night-club with its fusty, artificial atmosphere and its greedy entertainers, but in a dance-hall of the people, as she might have sat in a hall used for similar purposes in Neuilly or Naples or Innsbruck, but with what a difference! For here every individual effort was devoted towards the expression of electricity and living movement. Each dancer gave as serious an attention to his beautiful vocation as if he were in training for some great good game, and the colour of the participants, too, added attraction to the spectacle. This lithe African beauty, shading from light tan, through golden bronze, to blue-black, these boys and girls with woolly hair, these boys and girls with hair ironed out and burnished, themselves imparted to their savage pastime a personal fascination which was a rich ingredient in its quality.

☀ PARTIES ☀

It is kolossal, kolossal, cried the Gräfin, enraptured, clapping her hands together in her enthusiasm.

King Swan nodded his luke-warm approval, while Roy apparently was utterly unaware of the madness by which he was surrounded. Every now and again he helped himself to a draught from the flask which he had brought with him.

The dancing on the floor was perpetual, for one of the two bands was always playing. Wilder and wilder the couples became in their abandon, individuals separating one from the other to indulge in breath-taking displays of virtuosity and improvisation, and then joining again in double daring, until the scene resembled, to the spectator, an infinitely arranged chaos, and, to the participants, became that perfect expression of self so often denied human beings. Just when the tension for observer and dancer alike was becoming unbearable, the band would modulate the rhythm into that of a slow waltz, and violent energy was succeeded by lazy languor.

Presently, gazing this way and that, through and beyond the symmetrical disorder, the Gräfin spied Rilda at a table down the hall, somewhat removed from her own, with Siegfried, Midnight Blue, and Kim Skene. Occasionally, during those moments of intense and thrilling silence which occur spasmodically in Negro jazz music she could hear Rilda's mirthless, hollow laugh. Roy, impervious to the ribald sound of brass and bladder, heard it too and, after giving one quick, nervous glance over his shoulder in the direction of Rilda's table, frowned, and abruptly strode off to the men's toilet.

The Gräfin sighed. What can I do? she demanded. He's gone off to sniff coke. I wish I could stop it.

Once a snow-bird, always a snow-bird, was King's sententious summary of the situation. Only death'll stop it.

Sighing again, the Gräfin once more devoted herself ardently to the spectacle spread before her. A tall, brown man with fuzzy hair pressed forward almost in a kneeling posture, snapping his fingers at his partner, while she, twenty feet away, symbolically pushed him back with graceful hands. Unexpectedly, through the maze of dancers, the Gräfin recognized Noma Ridge dancing the Lindy Hop in almost Negroid fashion with a lanky, dark boy with laughing, lovable countenance, and prominent ears.

Dja see Noma Ridge dancing? Roy inquired, returning to the table.

Noting that the boy was once more wide awake and that his eyes glittered with excitement, the Gräfin mused aloud: What a wonderful partner she has! I wonder if he could teach me?

Adele, you *be*-have, Roy admonished her affectionately. I won't have you going 'round cracking your legs.

Donald Bliss and Simone Fly, who had just ascended

the stairs, passed the table. Although Simone had regained a limited use of her limbs in the interval since she had left Rosalie's, she still staggered. Her face was now an ugly shade of green with two spots of carmine daubed high on her prominent cheek-bones, her mouth a magenta splotch.

Hello, 'dele, she greeted the Gräfin. Haven't I been telling you 'twas marvellous? Is it or isn't it?

Marvellous! the Gräfin agreed.

Simone stood with her thumbs in the position they might assume were she wearing suspenders and were they inserted behind them, her head thrown back at an angle at which one might expect it to drop off, and her feet so far apart that she looked as if she were about to do the split.

I ask you, isn't it marvellous? she repeated interrogatively.

Donald winked at Roy and patted him on the head.

Roy'll sell the Sherry-Netherlands before the night is over, he said to the Gräfin. Then, to King Swan: Don't you ever work? How does the public ever expect to get 'round in New York if you laze like this?

Quit ridin' me, the chauffeur whined. I drove the madame and Roy up here an' I'll drive 'em back. Besides, he added, there are twenty-six thousand, nine hundred and ninety-nine other cars out in New York tonight.

Counted 'em, eh?

189

King Swan, disdaining to reply, knocked his cigarette ashes into the cuff of his trousers and blew his nose violently into a purple handkerchief with the head of Gloria Swanson printed in the white centre.

Donald led Simone to the dance-floor and presently they were giving an extremely good exhibition of how the Lindy Hop can be danced by white novices. Their version was a cross between a minuet and a tarantella, but they were obviously amused by it. Fortunately, enjoyment in dancing does not depend on efficiency.

Don's always ridin' me, King Swan complained to the Gräfin with a grin.

Cut it, snarled Roy, showing his teeth like an angry wolf. Quit dishing Don. He's reg'lar.

Ease it, kid, growled King. I ain't dishin' nobody.

The Gräfin laid a faintly admonitory hand on Roy's shoulder. Roy, behave, she adjured him. I want to watch the dancing.

The band was playing the St. James Infirmary. Midnight Blue, with Kim Skene, passed the table, and again Noma, with her dark, lanky partner.

We won't fight, ma'am, the chauffeur assured her. I know what's the matter with the kid.

I ain't too goddam sure . . . began Roy when his attention was diverted by something he saw on the floor: Rilda, in her riding-habit, crop in hand, dancing in the arms of Siegfried.

The dirty bastard! he muttered.

Hush, the Gräfin pleaded. Do get better tempered, Roy. Please pour me out a drink now, if you have any left in your flask.

Scowling, he obeyed her and then, quite suddenly, caved in, cringing.

I'm sorry, Adele, he said, and his eyes begged her forgiveness more than the words.

All right, Roy. It's all right. . . She patted him on the shoulder.

King Swan grinned and waved his hand across his face in a manner to indicate that there was very little he didn't understand. Then Hamish joined them and sat down in an empty chair by their table.

I'm looking for Rilda, he said. I've got the most enormous news.

Roy pointed her out. There she is, he cried, with that . . .

I'll wait till she stops dancing. I've just received a radio. . . Rilda probably will find one at home. . . David's getting in tomorrow on the Bremen.

Well that is nice, the Gräfin, utterly delighted, remarked. Isn't that nice, Roy? Now you won't have to go away.

David . . . Roy's pallor increased and he was seized with a most violent fit of trembling as he spoke this name as if it were a fetish, a formula, even a blood-rite. . .

Don't tell Rilda, please, Hamish, he begged, after a moment's pause.

Don't be silly, Roy . . . Hamish looked at the boy in astonishment. . . Of course, I've got to tell her.

The saxophone was playing such a strenuous rôle in the band's performance of the St. James Infirmary that it was necessary to shout to make oneself heard.

Certainly, Roy dear, he's got to tell Rilda, the Gräfin agreed. Besides, she'll surely find a radio of her own when she goes home. It's the uppies, she whispered to Hamish. Don't mind him. Did you bring a flask? she asked aloud.

Surely. Hamish produced his flask and poured another drink out for the Gräfin, King, and Roy.

Don't tell Rilda, Roy repeated, balefully fatalistic, his eyes staring unnaturally. Cut it, see! She's out there now dancing with that big heinie. Maybe . . . Well, I don't want David to find out about it, that's all. I know what David wants. He wants that guy dead. Lots o' times he asked me . . .

King Swan winked at Hamish. The Gräfin watched the dancers.

There, there, Roy . . . Hamish's tone was soothing and gentle . . . it'll be all right. Don't you worry.

To hell with you! the boy cried. I'm going to kill him. David wants me to. He said so.

At this instant the music stopped and Hamish stood up and signalled to Rilda before she should be carried away by the rhythm of the next tune. She waved her hand in reply and with Siegfried came over to the table.

Ignoring the presence of King Swan and Roy, who did not rise to greet her, she spoke to the Gräfin and Hamish. Siegfried remained a little to one side.

What do you want of me, Hamish? Rilda demanded impatiently, nervously switching her leg with her crop.

Hamish gazed into her tired eyes, observed her twitching eyelids.

Enormous news, Rilda dear, Hamish explained. Radio. You'll find one yourself at home undoubtedly. David. To-morrow. On the Bremen.

David! She tottered and would have fallen, had not both Hamish and Siegfried sprung forward to support her.

A moment later she said, Siegfried, I've got to go home at once.

Roy was on his feet facing her.

No, you don't, he cried. Not so easy.

The band was playing a waltz. The couples floated by languidly.

Roy dear, sit down, please, and keep still, the Gräfin pleaded with him.

I can take care of myself, Rilda announced contemptuously. She was standing alone now, a little apart from Siegfried.

Inflamed by Rilda's retort, Roy did not pay the slightest

heed to the words of the Gräfin. It was improbable, indeed, that he had heard them.

You and your guy! Roy cried. You'll get yours. You leave David alone. You stay away from David.

Rilda swayed slightly, like a willow-tree in a breeze, as she said in a deadly calm tone: If I were you, I'd let David choose his own vices.

Shut up, Roy, Hamish advised the boy testily. You don't know what you're talking about.

I ain't goin' to talk no more, the boy responded grimly.

Suddenly, before anybody could have an inkling of his purpose, he sprang forward, upsetting a chair. The knife flashing in his uplifted hand was buried a second later in Siegfried's breast. Without a groan or a cry of any sort, the blond giant crumpled, an ignoble heap on the floor. Action in the group was paralyzed for an instant. They were too amazed to be certain they had actually witnessed this scene. Before the dancers had time to collect around the wounded man, lying in a pool of blood, Roy had made a bound towards freedom. No one attempted to bar his passage until he arrived at the head of the staircase, when the cry of Murder! arose and a great black man headed the chase after the fugitive. Pausing a second to look back at his pursuers, Roy stumbled, and fell headlong, with a shriek of terror, to the very bottom of the flight of steps. The great black man looked down, then held up his hand to stop the music.

✳ *FIFTEEN* ✳

A cloudy early morning with a misty rain falling. A dismal, chilly group gathered on the North German Lloyd docks in Brooklyn. Passengers, awakened before dawn, now dumped into New York to struggle with the customs officers. Rilda, still in her riding-habit, her boots muddy, crying, looking ill, tired, and discouraged, with traces of a hangover, sitting on a trunk beside David, a very spruce and spick-and-span David in a new English suit. David's open luggage being examined by an inspector.

Poor Rilda, David said, stroking her hand. Poor girl, you've had a helluva night. No sleep at all?

None, David. They kept at us, the Gräfin and me, till nearly dawn, asking the same questions over and over again.

It's all my fault, Rilda, David announced with despair. If I didn't actually tell the boy to do it, I suggested it. I've simply got to face the fact: it's all my fault.

But I tell you, darling, Siegfried won't die. He was badly stabbed, but he won't die. All the doctors say that.

Can't say I'm glad, David replied. I hate him. It doesn't improve the situation. Roy's dead, isn't he? And he died trying to please me.

Is this here a new bathrobe? the inspector demanded, lifting a white velvet burnous embroidered in gold.

Certainly not, David replied. Can't you see it's full of cigarette burns? That kid loved me, he went on to Rilda, and I let him down.

Please, David, she pleaded, you mustn't feel so badly. I'm sure dope would have finished him off soon anyway.

What's in the papers?

It all happened too late for the morning papers. I dare say the afternoon papers will print plenty.

Very quietly and distinctly he spoke the thought in his mind: They'll look for a motive, you know.

David, I'm sorry, desperately sorry. . . Tears glistened in Rilda's tired eyes. . . It *is* a mess, isn't it? But I don't think the papers will find out much. The Gräfin is loyal, oh, so loyal! She's a wonderful woman, David. Hamish won't tell, or Donald, or Simone, or even Noma . . . Of course, she added, speaking the thought in *her* mind, I can't vouch for Rosalie . . .

Oh, I'll fix Rosalie all right. Poor kid! Poor little Roy.

The Gräfin's been wonderful, David, I can't tell you how wonderful. She was so brave last night, and *careful:* nobody could have been more careful. They couldn't shake her story. And one night she stayed with me, David, a terrible night when I went to pieces and wanted to kill myself. I couldn't stand it, your being away, David.

I've been a beast to everybody, David admitted, including myself.

Are these shirts new? the inspector inquired, looking up from his unenviable occupation.

Certainly, David replied chillingly, you'll find them in my declaration.

Oh, sure.

I'll never forgive myself, never, David went on to Rilda, for this rotten idea of mine of going away. Fear, that's what it was, fear. I couldn't face the thought of staying on at home and straightening things out where they needed to be straightened, *inside me*. No, I had to run away with the futile, cowardly hope that a miracle would happen. I *was* jealous of Siegfried. I admit it. I wanted him dead. I want him dead now. If he died, it would be my fault. I willed it. It is certainly my fault that Roy killed him, or tried to kill him, and Roy himself would be alive today if he hadn't done that.

But why do you feel that way about Siegfried, David? He really means so little . . . just a symbolic excuse.

That's just it! I wanted somebody to die as a symbol of my jealousy. You chose the victim and I accepted him.

The customs inspector was chalking the luggage.

O.K., he announced.

I think we can go, announced Rilda. As they rose to depart, she timidly sought his hand and retained it. You can't be sure of these things, she assured him, as they strolled towards the exit, followed by the porter who had piled the trunks and bags together on his truck. It is probably fate that Roy should die last night, and whatever you did, he would die anyway.

Dear Rilda, David said, and repeated still more affectionately, *Dear* Rilda. Then, Where's Hamish?

I asked Hamish not to meet you. You don't mind, do you? I wanted to see you first alone so that we could talk.

I'm glad he isn't here, David replied, frowning. That's something else. I can't look Hamish in the face. In London I had Irene. I didn't mean to tell you, but now that I've killed Roy I might as well tell you everything. What a miserable rotter I've been, Rilda!

Rilda's face was scarlet. Forget about Roy, she advised him. He's not worth remembering.

The funny thing is I've forgotten about Irene. I can't remember a single detail. I must have been very drunk. All I know is what she told me after.

Taxi, sir? inquired the porter.

Yes, David replied.

Maybe she was lying, Rilda suggested without conviction.

I don't know. I can't remember anything about it at all.

In the taxicab a little later she kissed him on the mouth.

It's so good, David, to have you all by myself for once, she sighed. Presently, she added, I forgot. Your mother's coming today.

He groaned. Dear mother. I can't face her cheerfulness today. How did she know . . . ?

She didn't, David. She just wired she was coming. When I received her wire I wasn't expecting you and I wasn't expecting Roy to stab Siegfried either. . . I might have wired her this morning, I suppose, but that would have been too late. She was on her way.

I'll never get over it. Never. Poor Roy! It was all my fault.

David, you musn't go on like this. You'll make yourself ill. After all, he was a little rotter.

He loved me.

David, that's just the trouble. Everybody loves you.

He groaned. I want a drink, Rilda, he said. I want a drink frantically. I haven't had a drop today yet. I wanted to get off the boat sober, for once . . . but now, well, I want a drink the worst way.

Do you want to stop at a speakeasy?

I guess I can wait till we get home. There won't be anything decent open at this hour. But this is a helluva long drive.

She pressed his hand. I hate it about Irene, she admitted.

Maybe it didn't happen, David said. Anyway, I hated it about Siegfried . . .

Rosalie . . . Rilda's face was hard.

Good God, Rilda, he interrupted her, are we going to begin all over again? Didn't it do *any* good for me to go away? Did I crucify myself in vain? Are we going to do nothing but torture each other always? Why?

Rilda kissed him again. I'm sorry, David, she said softly. It's my fault. I shouldn't be this way, but Irene — well, you know that's nearly knocked me out. It seems so futile, and so rotten to Hamish, and so rotten to me.

I agree with you, he replied soothingly. We've just got to forget the whole goddam mess and begin over. I suppose there'll be an inquest, he added.

Sure to be, she responded. Oh, David, I'm so sorry. Hamish is doing what he can with his lawyer and money . . . The newspapers . . . well, I don't see what they can say.

I don't give a damn about the newspapers and neither do you, Rilda. What we want is each other, whole or . . . he smiled bitterly . . . mended. Christ, I'd like a drink.

She looked at him through her tears. It will have to be " mended," won't it, David? And perhaps, " just as good as new."

Eight reporters were waiting for them in the entrance-hall of their apartment-house.

Nothing to say, snapped Rilda. Perhaps Mr. Westlake . . . She indicated her husband.

Mr. Westlake! . . . The astonishment was general. . . We thought you were in Europe. There's a rumour that you and Mrs. Westlake have separated.

Just got back today on the Bremen, David replied, and you can see we're not separated.

What have you got to say about this case, Mr. Westlake? demanded one of the reporters.

I can't say much, boys, David replied. I don't know anything about it yet. Give me time.

The elevator carried them up to an apartment in confusion. The newspapers had kept the telephone bell ringing, but as Rilda had not returned after the catastrophe until now, the servants were actually ignorant of the whole affair, and had obviously spoken the truth when they declared they knew nothing whatever about it.

Rilda made for her bath. David made for the bar.

The bar-room was so arranged that it received the morning sun through a ceiling-tunnel of graduated circles of glass. In the afternoon the lighting was artificial. In the morning, therefore, yellow wall-panels alternated with silver, but in the afternoon, by an ingenious mechanical device, the yellow panels were reversed to become orange. The room was irregular in shape, but suggested the intention of a triangle, with the bar at the shortest side. Over the bar hung a water-color by Carl Sprinchorn representing two sailors standing by a bar. The stools and chairs were silver with white leather cushions and there were two tables of metal and glass.

On this gloomy morning, very little light sifted into the room. David pressed the button which flooded the place with an electrical illumination, removed a vase of calla lilies from the bar to a table, and mixed himself a strong drink.

A little later Hamish was announced, and presently put in an appearance.

Hamish! David embraced him and added, A swell home coming! What will you drink?

Anything, Hamish replied. It doesn't matter. I've been up all night, running from hospital to police-station and just now I've come from seeing the Gräfin. Adele's all in. I've never seen her tired before. I feel sorriest for *her,* David. You know she's taken up Roy pretty thoroughly since you went away.

What do the police make of it?

Insane behaviour of a coke-addict. . . Hamish lifted to his lips the tall glass of whisky, gin, brandy, and bacardi that David had absent-mindedly poured out for him, and drained half of it at one gulp. . . Siegfried was conscious this morning and he swore to the police there was no reason for the act.

Good old Siegfried! I'm beginning to like him. Is he going to live?

Every chance, Hamish assented bitterly, adding, The
Gräfin and I testified that the kid was full of dope.

Was he? David demanded solemnly.

He was, David.

And Rilda?

Rilda's all right. Out of it completely, I'm sure, especially now you're back at this providential moment. She
never was in it very hard. The story goes that she went out
dancing and her escort got stabbed by a drug-addict on
the rampage.

Rosalie won't do anything?

I don't think she can, but she's sore as hell. You see —
oh, David, it doesn't mean a thing: Rilda loves *you* — but
she dragged Siegfried away from Rosalie last night. I
think . . .

Hamish was seated on a stool. David, standing, faced
him from behind the bar.

You think before I get any drunker . . . David swal-
lowed a beaker of brandy . . . I'd better call up Rosalie.

Yes.

The telephone in the bar was concealed behind one of
the silver panels in the wall. David fumbled with the
mechanism.

I've forgotten how it works, he confessed.

Hamish reminded him.

Been here a lot, eh? David inquired in a bantering
manner.

Hamish was pale. Twice, David. I just remembered, that's all.

Don't protest too much. Do you also remember Rosalie's number?

It's Volunteer . . .

I know. David called the number.

Hello, Rosalie . . .

Who . . . ? David!

Yes, my dear.

When did you get back? Do you know about . . . ?

This morning. Yes. You weren't there, I believe.

I've been to the hospital. I know quite enough.

Dope-addict. Little rotter.

Uhuh, she assented doubtfully. No other motive?

Dear Rosalie . . .

Dear David . . . Are you coming to dinner tonight?

Certainly. With pleasure . . . *and there was no other motive.*

Replacing the receiver and pressing the knob that reversed the silver panel, David covered his eyes with his hands.

What else could I do, Hame? I'm in an impasse. My first night home and back to Rosalie's for dinner! My mother is coming today too.

Your mother!

Returning to his place behind the bar, David replenished their glasses.

Yes, my mother. Oh, that's all right. She won't mind this mess. She's a sport. Only I wish it wasn't just today she was arriving.

David, you're a wonderful person. Hamish's eyes expressed his admiration.

No, I'm not, Hame, I'm filthy, Hame. Rather a bounder. Hame, Irene and I . . .

I knew. Somehow I knew, but it doesn't matter, David. Irene and I have lived apart for a long time.

Hamish tapped the bar nervously with his forefinger.

I didn't know I did it, Hame. I swear to God, I didn't know I did it. I don't remember a thing about it. She told me afterwards. I was drunk, Hame, stinking.

The maid opened the door, and hesitated for an instant before speaking.

Well, Edith, what's the matter?

Mrs. Westlake is coming up, sir. Shall I show her into the drawing-room?

Mrs. Westlake? Good God, my holy mother! Bring her in here, Edith.

The maid left the room.

The bar, David? So early? Hamish, wondering, inquired.

The bar, Hame. My mother knows everything about me that I know about myself. That's why we get on so well. . . Do you forgive me, Hame? Will you ever stop hating me?

205

I don't hate you, David. Whatever you did I couldn't hate you.

You should, Hame. I'm . . .

Mrs. Westlake, astonishingly young for her forty-five or so years, burst into the room like a middle-western breeze and embraced her son with fervour.

My darling David, you're not drunk yet, I hope?

Almost, mother. I've even got an excuse today. Had a bad time. This is my best friend, Hamish Wilding.

Delighted, Mr. Wilding. She held out her gloved hand with a frank gesture.

Dearest, I just got back to New York this morning on the Bremen.

But, David, I didn't know you'd been away. . . I think I could drink a glass of sherry, if you could find a biscuit.

I'm so sorry, dear mother. I should have asked you. . . David poured out the sherry and then searched in a cupboard behind the bar until he hit on a tin of Peek-Frean's. . . You were in Honolulu when I sailed, he explained, and you know how I am about writing.

I know. I suppose you were drunk most of the time.

As she made this remark, Mrs. Westlake frowned ever so slightly.

Lousy, stinking, slammocky, slummocky, sozzly, mildewed, musty, bloody ginny all the time. I'm your only mistake, mother.

You're my favourite child. Your brother's such a bore.

Quit kidding me, mother, and please be nice to Rilda.

Mrs. Westlake regarded her son with an expression indicating astonishment. What *do* you mean? she demanded. Am I not always nice to Rilda? I feel immensely sorry for any woman who has to put up with you, wonderful as you are. Besides, I adore Rilda.

I know, mother, but . . .

Again Edith appeared at the door.

Mrs. Fly is coming up, she announced.

Oh, Simone! I hope she brings good news.

Mrs. Fly? inquired Mrs. Westlake.

Simone's another one of our intimate friends, David explained.

What do you suppose she can want this morning? Hamish demanded rhetorically.

Where's Rilda? Mrs. Westlake inquired.

Oh, Rilda . . .

Simone exploded into the room. She was still wearing the same blue and white crêpe dress she had worn the previous afternoon. Her face was greener than ever, her make-up coming off in streaks, her mouth a magenta blur where the paint had rubbed. Her close-fitting hat concealed the disarray of her hair.

I think it's all right, she cried, waving her arms wildly. I think Donald's fixed the police. We've been working all night. . . She stopped suddenly, regarding David and his mother with astonishment. . . I beg your pardon, she said, I didn't know . . .

My mother, David explained to Simone. Mrs. Fly, he explained to his mother.

Does she . . . ?

I was just about to tell her when you came in, David assured her. It's quite all right.

I hope it's quite all right, cried Simone. Good God, gimme a shot of Pernod, Hame. Blaaa! I didn't know you were back, David. . . Seating herself on a stool she leaned backwards over the bar until her head almost dropped. Righting herself, she went on: Such a night! Donald's been swell. He talked the police blue. Not too much water, Hame. That's right. . . Accepting the proffered glass, she sipped the contents gingerly. . . He told them about Roy. Just a little rotter. Nothing to worry about. No mother. No father. Orphan, Dope-addict. Dipsomaniac. Nymphomaniac. Mmmmm . . .

Not that!

Megalomaniac, everything, she continued triumphantly. They believed him. All true. They'd better. She threw up her arms and her glass bounced on the rubber floor.

Was he really an orphan? Hamish, curious, demanded.

My dear, make me another, please. Don doesn't know. The boy's never said a word about his genealogy. Don's never asked him. Roy never talked much. . . You know. Thanks.

She sipped her fresh drink with pleasure.

The bewildered Mrs. Westlake, with a half-eaten biscuit in her hand and an untouched glass of sherry before her on the table, at last rebelled.

Darling, she demanded, are you going to tell me what has happened?

In a minute, best of mothers. Then to Simone: You're sure Don's fixed it?

Sure's anything can be. You know what a drag he has with the police.

Good old Don.

Of course . . . Simone screwed up her nose and twitched her ear between two fingers . . . there's Rosalie.

David groaned. I think I've fixed *her*. I'm dining there tonight.

Tonight! Good God, David, that's irony for you, cried Simone. Now I know that Freud and those fifty million other German analysts can't be wrong. . . To Hamish: A dash of bitters, please.

David . . . Mrs. Westlake's tone was more peremptory.

Mother, it's a mess, a reasty, maggoty mess which, as usual, is the fault of your favourite and disorderly son who is therefore trying to the best of his ability to straighten it out.

It's no one's fault, Simone and Hamish cried out almost in unison.

A coupla people got killed last night, David went on.

Killed! In the excitement provoked by this word Mrs. Westlake dropped her biscuit and gulped down her glassful of sherry.

David, let me tell it, Hamish urged. You weren't there anyway. You see, Mrs. Westlake, he explained, a young boy under the influence of drugs stabbed a man last night. The man will not die, but the boy was killed while he was trying to escape.

But . . . ?

Hamish did not reply to this unuttered question.

Rilda was with the man who was stabbed, mother, David said very quietly.

I shall be *very* nice to Rilda, Mrs. Westlake promised.

I knew you would, mother.

At that moment, Rilda, after a bath and some futile attempt at hair-dressing and make-up, very pale, very tired, appeared in the doorway in a white and black chiffon dressing-gown.

My dear Rilda! Mrs. Westlake embraced her daughter-in-law.

Have they told you, mother?

It was a painful shock to listen to Rilda's voice.

Yes, dear, of course. It's all right.

Rilda, Donald has fixed everything. . . Simone kissed her.

Don't you want a drink, Rilda?

Yes, Hamish, please. I believe a shot of straight gin. Donald . . . ?

He's fixed the police, David reiterated, but there's still Rosalie . . . his tone became hollow . . . and so I'm dining with her tonight.

Rilda stood with her back against the wall, looking across the bar straight at her husband. You are going . . . ?

Rilda, be reasonable, advised Hamish.

She choked and sputtered out the words: If you are going to Rosalie's tonight, so am I!

That will be nothing new, David remarked coldly. Probably Rosalie already has told the butler to lay a plate for you.

✻ SIXTEEN ✻

Neither the police, nor the newspapers, nor the coroner's inquest were as bad as might have been expected. Donald, quite obviously, had " fixed " the former, the newspapers with thin copy to go ahead on growled for a few days about " imminent investigations," discussed the possibility of other prominent names from the Social Register being dragged into the case, and at least one of the tabloids printed a dubious photograph of Noma Ridge dancing the Lindy Hop with an unidentified companion, thereby launching this dance on its subsequent brilliant career in lower Manhattan, but that was about as far as journalism progressed in the matter. The inquest was a farce. Siegfried, in the hospital, had made out a deposition to the effect that his assailant was unknown to him and consequently could have had no possible motive for his act, while the Gräfin and Donald testified that the would-be killer was a drug-addict whom the Gräfin was attempting to cure.

By her German-American friends, however, more particularly by her paid companion, the Gräfin was not let off so easily. Fräulein Stupforsch's anxiety concerning the Gräfin's eccentric behaviour had been increasing from week to week and this public exposure — certain newspapers had printed snap-shots of the Gräfin leaving the inquest, with appropriate and saucy captions — afforded her the excuse she had been praying for to call upon those transplanted fellow countryfolk of hers who belonged to a sufficiently lofty social scale to undertake the reproof of the Gräfin. As that lady, however, had only recently made their acquaintance and had no further need for their society, she considered their interference an impertinence and told them so in violent and picturesque German. After she had enjoyed a number of these scenes and disposed of her cringing opponents, she delivered her ultimatum to a weeping Fräulein Stupforsch. She announced that she had wearied at last of having underlings bestow attention on her private affairs, and that even thirty years' faithful service was insufficient authority for the continued practice of this privilege. She concluded this session by presenting Fräulein Stupforsch with her passage back to Germany, together with a letter giving her the right to become a member in perpetuity of the pensioned colony at the Schloss in Silesia. Far from regarding her banishment as a punishment, Fräulein Stupforsch looked upon it as a happy solution of her difficulties, for despite a certain formal fondness for the noblewoman, created by years of propinquity, however unfamiliar, the paid companion was at so great a disadvantage with her slight knowledge of English and so alarmed by the old lady's whimsical conduct in America, that she had not enjoyed one good night's sleep since the ship had sailed by the Statue of Liberty in the harbour. She, therefore, thanked the Gräfin with quiet dignity and within a week was on her way to the Schloss von Pulmernl und Stilzernl.

Before Fräulein Stupforsch had been disposed of, the Gräfin, together with David and Donald, both staunchly devoted to her interests and both sharing at least a modicum of her sentiments in regard to the occasion, arranged for the proper burial of Roy Fern. David himself was not much concerned with what became of a body after death, but he realized, even before he had discussed the matter with the Gräfin, that ceremony would have meant a great deal to Roy and so he helped her to carry out an idea of a funeral with flowers and prayers and Church of England splendour, Roy laid in a violet coffin smothered in snowdrops and banked with royal ferns, and buried with episcopal pomp, including a train of choir boys, intoning Onward, Christian Soldiers, and acolytes swinging censers burning incense, in a bought cemetery plot with the promise of a proper tomb to follow. These three made the arrangements; these three executed them; these three were present at the last rites: no more, save the necessary attendants and celebrants. At her insistence, the Gräfin was permitted to pay all the expenses incident to this reverent mummery, which was enacted without a hitch, for, in spite of the publicity allotted to his story, no kinsman had come forward to claim Roy's remains. So far as could be ascertained, indeed, Donald had been entirely straightforward when he had described the boy as an orphan.

Her German friends disposed of, Fräulein Stupforsch deported, the police investigation dropped, and Roy buried, the Gräfin a little pathetically reflected that for the first time in her life she was entirely free of any tie or responsibility, pleasant or unpleasant. She was not certain that she should regard this condition as enviable, but however she might regard it she could not overlook the fact that the condition existed.

She was, on the whole, devoted to American life, an emotion largely brought about by the accident which had placed her almost immediately in a milieu which pleased her more than any of which she had hitherto been cognizant, and determining to become an American citizen — the fact that Germany was now a republic simplified her desire to make this break with an important past — she took out her first papers. This was not the unique alteration she made in her mode of living. She engaged Mattie, a companionable and sociable Negro maid who was sympathetic to a degree the Gräfin described to her friends by the word " poignant," and in Mattie's company and with her advice she visited several large shops and selected a new wardrobe. She did not go into mourning and she made no effort to appear younger, but she cherished an ambition to look more American or at least

like a German of a fresher vintage and to that end she dis-
carded her high, laced boots in favour of low shoes and her
stiff taffetas in favour of soft-coloured chiffons, cut in simple styles. She even laid aside her bonnets.

Also she moved. Her original hotel, certainly an excellent hostelry, with its huge rooms, thick carpets, and heavy
furniture, had been recommended by one of her German-
American friends. Craving more modernity, she transferred her trunks to a hotel-apartment with a bar, kitchen-
ette, an electric refrigerator which turned out ice-cubes
faster than she could use them, and a radio. It was a great
pleasure for the Gräfin to lie in bed and listen to Toscanini
or Amos 'n' Andy without going through the struggle of
being obliged to locate them on the air herself — an
anonymous operator downstairs did that. All that was required of the Gräfin was that she should plug in one of the
alternative stations.

The new apartment, the new maid, the new citizenship
were not enough. The Gräfin was obliged to select a successor to Roy, and that immediately, if she wished to
continue her career in the night-clubs, speakeasies, and Harlem dance-halls. Indeed, this necessity was more imperative than a maid. King Swan applied for the position, but
he failed to qualify, for several important reasons, either
with the Gräfin or Donald. The bootlegger's candidate for
the office was Freddie, his colourless (but for his red hair)
assistant, and the Gräfin eventually accepted him, though

with many misgivings, which proved to be well founded. The fact was that Freddie experienced so great an anxiety to keep the job and was so desirous of pleasing his new patron, that he constantly hovered about her, self-conscious and nervous, with his yes ma'ams and no ma'ams, even trying to anticipate her wishes, until the Gräfin was inclined to sigh for a more irregularly minded page. Freddie did not drink. While he was " working " he could scarcely be induced to smoke a cigarette. His only vice was the vice of assiduity and so, when the Gräfin returned to her apartment and her bed and he was free to do whatever he liked, he was actually too tired, as well as too unimaginative and too lacking in desire, to think of doing anything but to go to sleep himself. He was a poor boy who had gone through a long struggle and when luck came he appreciated it. If he were not very clever, at least he was efficient and conscientious. Unfortunately these qualities were anathema to the Gräfin: she had been surrounded by their possessors all her life. She required an amusing escort and Freddie would have satisfied her demands more fully had he been more inconsiderate of her feelings and governed by selfish desires. From red-haired Freddie she looked in vain for lapses, for evidence of secret vices, even for misdemeanours or simple errors of deportment. On the contrary, he was always attentive, punctual, and sympathetic, never lazy, obstinate, or loquacious. In other words he made every attempt to do what he conceived was expected of him, and for the most part he succeeded in this attempt. In fact, he possessed all the qualities desirable for a cup-bearer in a speakeasy and when Donald parted from him, he really believed he was making a sacrifice in favour of the Gräfin.

If that lady were not pleased, if, indeed, she felt keenly disappointed, at any rate she did not complain. Actually, she couldn't find it in her heart to do so. The boy was so sweet, so willing, so humble, she did not wish to hurt him by suggesting that he put a little more of his energy and waking thoughts into the invention of wicked and unexpected acts. Besides, he would not have understood her.

One night, after they had attended many cocktail parties and visited several other speakeasies, they had repaired to the Wishbone where Freddie, as was so often his habit in Donald's place, not only served the Gräfin, but also helped the new boy with the other customers. These included, in the large sitting-room, Midnight Blue with Kim Skene and, at another table, an unknown man, well-dressed and presumably English, who was playing one game of patience after another and consuming large quantities of Irish whisky. Beauty Butcher was performing very sentimentally Have a Little Faith in Me on the miniature upright piano and somehow the tune, the subdued atmosphere of the place, and Freddie's exemplary conduct, made the Gräfin feel old, as old as Erda, she began to believe,

and from some unconscious depths of her mind she
dragged forth the lines:

> Mein Schlaf ist Träumen,
> Mein Träumen Sinnen,
> Mein Sinnen Walten des Wissens.

And now, lulled by the music Beauty Butcher was playing
on the little piano, music so unlike Erda's that she wondered what had reminded her of Erda, the Gräfin recalled
some of the nights of operetta so long ago at the Theater
an der Wien, new wine nights at Rockenbauer's outside of
Vienna where she had flirted with and been teased by the
young lieutenants, Slibowitz and carp at Schöner's on
the Siebensterngasse, and melancholy band concerts in the
Prater where she had ridden around and around on her
black stallion Werther. It was strange, sometimes, she
reflected, how a few drinks and a banal tune would make
one sentimental and bring back memories of the lovely old
days. After all, what was life itself but a succession of contradictory moods and one's victory in life, like one's success at a party, depended on how one reacted to these
moods.

Wiping away a furtive tear, the Gräfin beckoned Freddie to join her, and enjoyed another sip of her gin-rickey.
After all, she assured herself, up to the time of Roy's
death, she had been happier in America than she had ever
been before in her life, and it was probably the very fulness

of this happiness which was responsible for the intensity of her sadness.

Midnight Blue, under cover of the music, was conversing in a low tone with Kim Skene.

I tell you, she assured him, I am sailing.

Beloved and darkest Midnight, what can I do without you?

Why don't you sail too?

Sometimes one can't do everything he wishes.

Kim, I'm sure you're rich.

I haven't a penny, darling.

What if I paid?

Darkest Midnight, in that case I would follow you to Tibet.

The Gräfin took in the import of this scene without overhearing the conversation. Midnight knew what she wanted and was willing to buy it. That was satisfactory and reasonable. . . Glancing down the hallway — the open doorway commanding a complete view of this artery was directly in her line of vision — she was startled to see Donald surreptitiously kissing Irma Oberhalter as he opened the outer door for her. So that too had happened. The Gräfin sighed. Well, probably Irma would be happier because of her assured unhappiness. It was, of course, unthinkable that she should marry Donald . . . unless . . . well, it didn't seem at all impossible that he might marry her. What would Friedrich think if he knew? . . . After all, why should they marry? Why was marriage desirable or even necessary? Her own marriage had only brought her stuffiness and boredom, castles and formal dinners. From the gaiety of her youth she had been plucked to become a wife — fortunately not a mother — and she had attended to the duties of her new occupation with as much grace as she could assume until the death of the Graf and even after. The Gräfin had never shirked responsibility. She believed she had been a good wife. Looking back, she could find nothing to reproach herself with, but she wondered a little if she could not reproach others. How different her life might have been if she had run away with one of those roguish lieutenants at Rockenbauer's during the new wine season. . . Beauty Butcher was playing With a Song in My Heart. . . Rilda and David, for instance, splendid people: she loved both of them, but wouldn't they have been happier unmarried? Would there then have been this terrific strain, this tension that tore them apart and held them together? . . . But it was love that caused this tension and not the law. She sighed again as she realized that marriage as a legal institution had very little to do with the question.

Do you want anything, ma'am? Freddie demanded, gazing at her with his deep-set, hazel eyes, like those of a frightened doe, so intently that she wondered if some time this boy would break her heart.

No, Freddie, I don't want anything, thank you.

Again she wiped the tears away, but she had already begun to believe they flowed on account of Freddie.

What's the matter then, ma'am? Can't I do something?

There's nothing the matter, dear Freddie, except I guess I must be too happy.

Maybe you miss Roy, the boy suggested simply.

She *did* miss Roy, more than anybody she had ever known and lost. That was why she had been dreaming, in this incongruous environment, of the old days and the old places. She missed the excitement connected with Roy's presence, his unaccountable remarks and acts, his selfishness, his frank preference of David to herself, his fragile and dissipated appearance. He had begun to seem to her like a son, the kind of son she would have preferred and she could never forget that it was Roy who had introduced her to her favourite aspects of New York life.

Standing beside the piano, cigarette in the corner of his mouth, Donald talked to Beauty Butcher while he played.

I guess Kim's found another sucker.

You think she'll take him on?

Ke-rist, she took him on weeks ago, but he's playing her for the grand tour, and she's going to give it to him. It's these hard-hearted queens that fall the softest for the gigolos. Seems a shame after old man Crane coughed up his lungs for him.

Old man Crane? Beauty unaccountably was playing the scene at the fountain from Pelléas et Mélisande.

Sure. Malvina's father. To get rid of him he pays him a hundred grand and then Malvina throws herself away on Buddy Parsons, and the old man will always have to support *him*. Some people don't know no luck.

The doorbell rang and with a great rattling of chains and shooting back of bolts, the new boy let in Simone, rather sober.

She patted Beauty on the head, said Hello to Donald, and passed on to the Gräfin's table, where she seated herself.

I'm worried about Rilda and David, she began at once.

Has anything happened? the Gräfin anxiously inquired.

Same old thing, Simone replied, clutching the floor behind her chair with her toes, awarding her protruding knees an excessive sharpness. I thought it would stop after David had been away. It's worse. . . All because David went to dinner at Rosalie's the night he came back. He had to go to get Rosalie to behave about Roy and Siegfried. We know that, all of us. So does Rilda. She knows it better than any of us. Anyway it made her wild.

I haven't seen them together, the Gräfin admitted. David has been very kind to me . . . and so has Rilda.

They aren't ever together any more . . . except at parties. That's where they see each other. It's just what it used to be. David is blind, stinko, most of the time, and so is Rilda. Freddie, get me an old-fashioned, will you, like a dear?

223

❋ PARTIES ❋

Freddie got up at once to do as he was requested. Beauty Butcher was playing My Fate is in Your Hands.

I'm very sorry, said the Gräfin. I love them both.

They love each other, Simone went on, desperately, passionately. They cling to each other like barnacles cling to rocks, but they want to hurt each other all the time to test their feeling. . . Suddenly she thrust her legs in front of her, heels wide apart. . . Gimme some of your drink, Adele, while I'm waiting.

Certainly, Simone. . . The Gräfin pushed her gin-rickey across the table. Is Siegfried out yet?

Oh, yes, he's discharged from the hospital, and from Rilda's life too. She hasn't gone back to *that*.

I don't think his family would let him go back to her. They'll whisk him away somewhere, said the Gräfin. She laughed, as she added, probably he's had his lesson.

I wonder, Simone mused, as she sipped her gin-rickey, if there was ever anything between those two. . . Sometimes I think not.

Recalling the night she had spent as chaperon at Rilda's, the Gräfin asserted fervently, I am sure not.

Thank you, Freddie, said Simone, as the boy returned with her drink. You'd better bring Adele another rickey because I've made a dent in her last one.

Yes, ma'am, he replied and hastened to obey her.

Beauty Butcher was playing You Mean Something to Me.

224

I'll do it, Midnight Blue whispered to her companion. I can't go without you.

Beloved and darkest Midnight . . . Kim stroked her hair lightly and then bent forward to kiss her lightly.

Is Simone looking at me? Beauty inquired of Donald who still hovered over the piano.

No. Why?

Well . . .

God, man, she can't look at you all the time. . . He returned to the more interesting subject of Kim: That well-brushed gigolo is going on the grand tour all right. The movie dame is reaching in her pockets this minute.

Simone dropped a glass, spluttered out a Blaaa, and cried, Beauty, come on over. Kim was now kissing Midnight in a more satisfactory manner. The Gräfin watched the unknown English gentleman stagger towards the door. As Donald opened it, to let him emerge, David's voice could be heard from the stairs.

Hello, Don. Here we are, Hame and me. Ready for whoopee and yellow hair and gin and sin and what have you.

The pair entered, as drunk as any one had ever seen them.

❋ SEVENTEEN ❋

It is possible that Mrs. Alonzo W. Syreno no longer actually desired to possess David, but it is more likely that she was sufficiently foresighted to perceive the risk she would run by attempting to prolong their illicit conduct. She cherished no ambition to be labelled a fast woman and she was quite aware that while Rilda might overlook or be ignorant of certain episodes in her European career, she would certainly assume a different attitude regarding her behaviour in New York. Moreover — and this probably was the motive that influenced her most strongly — she had no intention of throwing away the social advantages that might fall to her through association with David's " set " — the word naturally was her very own and would, indeed, have been almost meaningless to David. Rich, with an apartment on Park Avenue, she determined to entertain her new acquaintances until they would be forced to recognize her seriously and permanently as one of themselves.

The apartment occupied two floors and was so enormous that she sometimes wondered how two people ever lived alone in it. For one, it was ridiculous. There were twelve bedrooms, a colossal drawing-room, a library, two sitting-rooms, two dining-rooms, a reception-room, and a gymnasium. A certain preserve-closet, previously referred to, figured among the lesser cubby-holes. Only two of the bedrooms had ever been utilized, and a good many of them, including that formerly slept in by her husband, Mrs. Alonzo W. Syreno had never even entered. The apartment had been furnished in " perfect taste " by an English decorator who had rid himself of a good many pieces of furniture, of which, until this opportunity offered, he had given up all hope of disposing. As for pictures, he had completely cleaned out, at an amazing price, his sup-ply of pseudo-Romneys, suspicious Gainsboroughs, and Lawrences with fragile histories, so that he had been obliged to cable to England for more, thus creating a brisk boom in trade for the dealers in the Caledonian Market. Nevertheless, the result of this furnishing was not unpleas-ant either to eye or buttocks. The place looked all right, and if one sat down, he sat down in comfort. There was not, however, in the whole apartment one single touch to remind one of Mr. or Mrs. Alonzo W. Syreno. It was indeed fortunate that it had never entered Mrs. Syreno's pretty head to buy an objet d'art or an article of furniture, so that the pure effect the apartment gave of resembling a permanently uninhabited English house had never been destroyed, especially as this effect was admired and fostered by the butler.

On a certain evening after dinner several of Mrs. Alonzo W. Syreno's new acquaintances — she believed them to be her friends — were gathered in her drawing-room, seated in a circle, for all the world like an old-fashioned minstrel show grouping, on the Chippendale and Sheraton and Heppelwhite and Jacobean fauteuils, settles, benches, stools, and couches with which the place abounded. In addition to the hostess, the circle included Rilda and David, not sitting together, Hamish, Simone Fly, Rosalie Keith, the Gräfin and Freddie, Beauty Butcher, and Peter Rokeby. They had all dined so well that the gallons of cocktails consumed before dinner, the Heidsieck 1915 they had consumed at dinner, and even the whisky and soda they were consuming at present, had as yet made only a slight impression on the group.

By way of entertainment Mrs. Syreno had provided a clairvoyant of some fame. Claire Madrilena described her, according to report, as a prodigious genius who turned the guts of the soul inside out, and Noma Ridge had confessed that the woman had presented her with perfect characterizations — that is as perfect as Noma's memory would lead her to believe — of her thirty-six latest lovers, or perhaps temporary consorts would be a more exact designation.

The clairvoyant, a Negro lady neatly dressed in a blue serge tailored suit, with a blue felt hat and a beige blouse, sat at one point in the circle, facing the group. She had an interesting oval face the colour of coffee with cream in it, with large, staring, brown eyes, behind glasses. She sat for some moments in silence, and so, save for a few whispered comments, did the others. Nor did she at once concentrate on any member of the group. Her eyes roamed restlessly and apparently inattentively from the fire to Gainsborough's Green Boy over the mantelpiece, and again to the Persian carpet. At last they settled, not unmalignantly, on Beauty Butcher, and the clairvoyant began to speak in a clear, well-placed, resonant, bold, self-possessed, contralto voice.

You are not well, she began not too encouragingly. I know you are not well, because I am well and when I look at you I feel sick. You have trouble with your stomach, don't you?

Her victim nodded.

Cirrhosis of the liver?

He nodded again.

And with your head. You have head-aches?

He nodded for the third time.

I knew it. I don't feel well. When I say that I mean *you* don't feel well. I am *you* now. I don't feel a bit well. Not a bit. Oh, I am so tired, so very tired. . . She cupped her cheek in her palm and rocked her head, staring, staring. . . You must take care of yourself. Not enough sleep. Too late hours. Too much to drink. Too much misdirected thought of self.

Wagging her head rapidly from side to side, suddenly her eyes fastened on Peter Rokeby.

Hungry! she hurled at him. I'm hungry. I mean *you're* hungry when I say that. I could eat all the time. I go from house to house eating and drinking. I eat here and I eat there. I ate two lunches today.

Oh, I say! the Englishman protested.

Two lunches! the seeress insisted.

This is really alarming, Hamish whispered to Simone.

It's awful! Blaaa! Simone stretched her legs wide apart and slumped back into the couch.

Hungry! Hungry! The pythoness gave her subject one last withering glance and passed on to the Gräfin.

A good woman — oh, so much goodness — a foreign woman, a foreign, good woman, a good, foreign woman. Oh, I feel so good! Oh, you make me feel so good! I don't believe anybody else in the room is so good! You are generous and charitable and kind and tolerant. I see you carrying baskets of turkey to the poor. Do you carry baskets of turkey to the poor?

I don't think . . .

Of course, my dear, you wouldn't admit it, wouldn't admit it, wouldn't admit it. . . Her voice rose almost to a shriek and her yellow fingers clawed the air . . . but you are good. You've lost somebody very dear to you, haven't you?

A perceptible and unanimous shudder gave the circle a false semblance of harmony.

Yes, the Gräfin replied very quietly. She engaged one of Freddie's hands.

Oh, you are so good. Believe me, my dear, it will be all right. You will get what you want. You *must* get what you want. You are so good. Don't worry. Don't fret. Don't moan. You will get what you want. You are so good, so good. You will get what you want. . .

Closing her eyes, she wagged her head back and forth, until when her eyes reopened she turned them suddenly on Mrs. Alonzo W. Syreno.

Shallow! she hissed at her. Shallow, vain, and silly. Mean little personality. No head. No heart. Nothing. Empty. Empty. Try to think of others. Try to give others some consideration. You do not love your husband. Nothing to love him with. Nothing . . .

I am sure . . . cried the squirming Mrs. Alonzo W. Syreno, leaning forward breathlessly, her cheeks flaming.

Wait! cried the prophetess, in the deep voice of authority. I was brought here to tell the truth, paid to tell the truth. I would prefer to be in my bed at home, but I have been brought here and paid to tell the truth.

I've heard enough, Mrs. Alonzo W. Syreno protested. You'll get paid all right, but I've heard quite enough.

We haven't, David assured her.

No. No. Tell ours. Blaa! The others agreed with him.

I must have complete silence, the clairvoyant said. I cannot see souls when there is noise. I must have silence.

She sat very still herself, fingering the catch on her hand-bag.

The very idea! grumbled the indignant Mrs. Alonzo W. Syreno.

Sh! This from Simone who placed her full glass carefully on a small table beside her.

Turning her deep gaze on Hamish, squinting, the woman regarded him for nearly a minute.

You do not know yourself, she brought out at last. You don't know where you are, or who you are, or what you are, or what you want. You are not unhappy, you are miserable. You do not understand.

Good God! was Simone's involuntary exclamation, as she exchanged swift glances with David and dared to take a sip of her drink. David immediately averted his eyes.

What nonsense! cried Mrs. Alonzo W. Syreno. I can't stand any more of it. I'll come back when it's over. . . She rose and left the room.

The seeress seemed oblivious to this interruption. Wildly she went on pouring out the words: You constantly sacrifice your own desires to satisfy those of your friends. You are generous. You don't know how generous you are, because you don't know what it is you give away. You are a miserable creature and I pity you very much. You want so much so badly, and you do not know what it is you want. . . Poor, dear creature, poor boy, I would like to help you, so many people would like to help you, but we do not know what it is you want.

The clairvoyant smiled convulsively, sighed, and then began to wag her head again. There was complete silence, complete attention. Presently she turned her eyes on Rosalie whose own glance held no candour.

Jealous, the oracle proclaimed, a jealous woman. Can't bear to have any one else have anything. Want it all yourself. Don't want anybody to have even what you don't want. Jealous, but you're not so bad really. Every now and then you do somebody a good turn. Do more of 'em. Be good. Be good like the foreign lady. . . She nodded at the Gräfin. . . They say, Be good and you'll be happy. It's true. Be good and you'll be happy. Be good and you'll be happy. . . She droned off into a sing-song once more.

Now she was looking at Simone.

A wonderful woman. A brave woman. You have to struggle with yourself and others, but you give more than you receive. You think the best of everybody and wish the best to everybody and give everybody anything you have. Sometimes you wonder why you don't get more in return. Wait. Have patience. You will get everything your heart desires. It's all coming to you. You are a brave woman. You struggle, but you will get what you want.

Blaaa! Simone dropped her glass at last.

Now, as the butler swiftly crossed the room to clean the debris from the carpet, the seeress moaned and rubbed her forehead.

Probably, you're tired, suggested Rilda. Probably you'd better stop now and not do any more.

No, I'm not tired, the soothsayer cried in a strong, vibrant voice. I'm not tired. I'm tortured. Fire and flame, I see, and suffering. Martyrdom. Hate and love. Steel and blood. Spurs and instruments of torture. Whips and thorns. Burning at the stake is nothing to what I see. The crucifixion is nothing to what I see. Torture for you. Torture for him. Fire and flames and knives and gutters running with blood . . .

Stop, please! Rilda cried. . . Her voice was choked and husky. . . I've heard quite enough. I don't want to hear any more. You've said enough, you horrible woman. . . Then, in a calmer voice, to the butler, May I have a drink of Scotch, please.

As the man fulfilled Rilda's desire, Mrs. Alonzo W. Syreno appeared in the doorway. Her entrance was so timely that it was apparent she had been listening.

You see . . . she began, and shrugged her shoulders. Then, more fiercely, she addressed the clairvoyant: I told you to go.

I do what I'm paid to do, the Sibyl replied proudly. I am paid to speak and I speak the truth. When it is necessary

I cut with a sword. I tell the truth. I do not snivel and grovel.

Accepting the filled glass from the butler's extended tray, Rilda drained the contents at one gulp.

You have been a little shameful, Rilda, David remarked. After all, we asked her to stay.

Very collectedly, the woman rose from her chair, put her bag under her arm, bowed inclusively to the company, and walked out of the room, followed by Mrs. Alonzo W. Syreno. They could be heard conferring in the hall. The group in the drawing-room was self-conscious and silent. At last the outer door was heard to open and close, and Mrs. Alonzo W. Syreno returned to her guests.

She made the gesture of washing her hands.

We're rid of *her,* she remarked.

David's despairing glance followed the direction taken by the departed clairvoyant.

I think you were wrong, Rilda, he said, not to listen. There might have been something.

David! . . . She joined him at once. . . Let's stop her. Let's get her back. I'm sorry I behaved so badly.

Racing to the hallway, they opened the outer door. The entrance lobby was used by no other tenant. There were only two doors, one opening on the apartment of Mrs. Syreno, the other on the elevator. The room was empty. David rang for the elevator attendant. When he appeared,

Rilda asked him if he could call back the woman he had just taken down.

The boy was sleepy. He had an appearance, indeed, of having just been awakened.

I ain't taken nobody down, he said. This car ain't been up for the last thirty minutes.

✻ EIGHTEEN ✻

Spring in New York is as attractive as spring in anywhere else, but her appearance has a peculiar effect on the
inhabitants of Manhattan Island. Every true Englishman
returns to England to enjoy the English spring, but when
the buds begin to burst and the birds begin to warble and
trill in the New York parks every real New Yorker longs
to travel. Hamish then was quite within the tradition when,
strolling up Madison Avenue on a heavenly spring day, he
was filled with nostalgia for the countries he did not belong in. The Sheffield plate and Georgian silver in one
window, the Venetian glass in a second, the Russian samo-
vars in a third, and the Czechoslovakian peasant blouses in
a fourth, made him sigh in turn for Mayfair, the Grand
Canal, the Kremlin, and the Moldau, and it occurred to
him that he should immediately book his passage to one
of these places.

He began to whistle the tune of Why was I born? but
the sentiment of the unsung words did not come to his
memory until he had rounded out the cadence when, rather
bitterly, he realized the application he might make of
them. Here he was, twenty-five, separated from his own
wife, made a cuckold by his best friend, futilely and hope-
lessly in love with that friend's wife, and in love with that

friend. He lived without a plan, without thought of the future, with no occupation save the consumption of liquor, on a great deal too much money which came to him from dubious sources by way of a trust fund established by a loving father. Sometimes Hamish thought he would like to become a writer, like Edgar Wallace or Conrad, and he had considered, not very seriously, the possibility of accepting a position (which had not been offered to him) in a stockbroker's office. He was getting on; a career of drinking and drifting must stop at some date, he supposed: probably when he was fifty. He might then conceivably put off his decision in this matter for twenty-five years. Yet, as he walked up Madison Avenue on this bright spring day, he wondered. He was not accustomed to thinking, but the seeress at Mrs. Alonzo W. Syreno's had indicated to him the necessity, or at any rate the advantages, of ratiocination. On reflection he was not so sure there were advantages. On the whole, thinking merely served to depress him. The clairvoyant had declared that he did not know what he wanted. Well, aside from knowing that he wanted Rilda, he was aware that his other desires were comparatively feeble, and he could not possess Rilda and continue to know David, and not to know David was an unthinkable condition. His life then was governed to a degree he had never fully sensed before by David's acts and thoughts, a situation further complicated by the fact that apparently David often acted without thinking. . . At

Sixty-first Street Hamish struck off west towards the Park.

He had led a hell of a life, if a brief one, with Irene. Rilda and David tortured each other because they loved one another devotedly. Irene had actually hated him. He still could recall quite clearly that last night when, screaming in her fury, she had broken every breakable object in a hotel room in Boston — but he could not remember why they happened to be in Boston — and had departed in her nightdress, covered by a cloak. The next day she had sent for her clothes and he had never seen her again. At the time he had thought he would never want to, but later a vague ache in his heart told him that he missed something, were it only a habit. This feeling too disappeared in time, to awaken spasmodically on those strange occasions when some perfume or feminine movement or even a dress reminded him of Irene. He had never tried to get a divorce, although that procedure would have been simple since she had deserted him to live in England, because he had never made any plans that depended on a divorce. Indeed, he was beginning to learn that he never made any plans at all. He loved only David and Rilda, his plans depended on theirs, and when David went away he was lost. He did not know what to do with himself, or even what to do with Rilda.

Hamish was certain that David knew everything about himself, understood even the strange necessity, the queer perversity, which made him drink, which made him sadistic, but Hamish did not understand David, any more than he understood himself, did not understand his actions, or their motives, or even that pervasive charm which made him so frightfully attractive to all who came within the range of his personality.

Hamish sighed as he seated himself on a bench in the Park. The sky was very blue over his head and the buds on the willow-branches by the pond were bursting under the warm rays of the sun. He watched the children playing about on the gravel-paths while their nurses chatted with an ancient policeman and an old man in a brown derby hat fed crumbs to the sparrows. The day was warm, the scene was a pleasant one and should have proved satisfactory in itself, but there was something about it that created in Hamish the desire to go to Italy, and yet he couldn't go to Italy without David, and what David intended to do, nobody could be sure.

As regards human relationships in general, the winter had not been very clarifying to Hamish. The lovable people were more lovable, perhaps, and the hateful people more hateful, but on the whole everything seemed as mixed and muddled and unreasonable to him as it had at the beginning of the fall . . . as it had always seemed. There was predominantly, of course, the case of Roy, whose curious but unimportant personality had disturbed all those who had come in contact with him. His death — perhaps

because he had died a martyr to a perverse sense of loyalty
— had had far-reaching effects: it had made David know
regret for the first time, it had created a certain wistful-
ness in the hitherto gay Gräfin, it had even driven a recovered Siegfried back to Germany. The whole tone of living,
indeed, seemed to have been depressed. The winter had
been violent, exciting, sometimes even amusing, but spring
appeared to be gentle and melancholy like Massenet's
Elégie played by a brass band in the vicinity of the fountain of the Medicis in the Luxembourg Gardens, or the last
scene of Der Rosenkavalier, or Tatjana's air from Eugene
Onegin, or the March of the Toys from the Babes in Toy-
land, or the hands of Mei-Lan-Fang, or his voice, which
Claire Madrilena had described as " like a sea-gull calling
out to the captain of a lost ship," or Duse in The Lady from
the Sea, or late autumn in the Berkshires, or summer in the
country near Tours, or Helen Morgan sitting on a piano,
or the flower gardens at Hampton Court, or the cradle
of the Duc de Reichstadt, or Daisy Miller, or Richard
Tauber singing An der Volga. At least Hamish, sitting
idly on a bench in Central Park this balmy spring morning, felt the New York spring was like that.

The sparrows hopped about after the crumbs the old
man in the brown derby was tossing on the path, the children ran from the knees of their nurses to the border of the
soft grass that was just beginning to show itself and then
ran back again, and a handsome, brawny stevedore, in

overalls, with Tiptoe Through the Tulips With Me printed
on the visor of his cap, passed whistling shrilly. As the sun
mounted higher in the sky, Hamish recalled with some
pleasure the many mornings when he and David had
abandoned the artificially lighted cabarets of Harlem to
drive in the bright sunlight through the Park, decked with
its pink and white plum and cherry blossoms and Judas-
trees, with their magenta boughs, the towers of the city
ahead of them rising pearly pink and mauve to an incredible height. More especially he recalled one such
morning when David from their open taxi had called out a
cheery Good morning to a corpulent gentleman riding a
roan stallion on the bridle-path and how, when the corpulent gentleman had ignored this salutation, David had instructed his chauffeur to cause the taxi to circle about again
and again so that wherever the drive crossed the bridle-
path and the rude and corpulent gentleman's trail, he
might continue to salute him with added epithets of a
more profane nature.

Feeling a little cool, for the heat of the season was not
yet excessive, Hamish rose to stroll once more, now towards Fifty-ninth Street where over the tops of the green-
ing trees myriad towers rose against the sky, creating an
amazing spectacle which confirmed his desire to go somewhere, were it only for the pleasure of coming back to New
York, a pleasure of which he never seemed to tire. Then
the cock on the Heckscher Building reminded him of the

storks of Strassbourg and Strassbourg reminded him of Germany and Germany reminded him of the Gräfin and he was shame-faced to remember that he had not called upon or seen the Gräfin for a week, this Gräfin who had adopted this country as her own and who, whatever others might do, was determined to stick out a New York summer, an experience, however agreeable, which Hamish had never yet enjoyed. Nevertheless, he reflected, whatever pleasure the Gräfin derived from living in New York was to some extent vitiated by the fact of Roy's death and the incompetency in certain essential respects of his successor, Freddie. Hamish determined therefore to look in upon the Gräfin this very afternoon.

It sometimes occurred to Hamish to wonder idly — and this morning was one of those occasions — why he had never married Simone. She was attractive in her strange, " paintable " way, and since her divorce had become kinder, softer and more pliable. Hamish recalled the night when she had cracked a twelve-inch, red-seal Caruso record over her husband's head. Time and suffering had made her more tolerant. Hamish believed that were she to be angry now she would be satisfied to employ a ten-inch Libby Holman for a similar assault. . . She would make an excellent wife for me. . . Hamish rolled the idea over in his mind. . . I'm sure we should get along famously. I couldn't marry Rosalie or Mrs. Alonzo W. Syreno or Noma, certainly not Noma — that would be like marrying an octopus. I would be swamped by Claire's personality. . . But perhaps Simone had confided her future to Beauty Butcher. Perhaps she had chosen him as her mate. He was, certainly, in her company a great deal, but Hamish believed this to be a matter of convenience. Beauty was useful; he could escort her to the theatre or to the speakeasy life she affected. It was, probably, a relationship no more serious than that. Still Hamish realized that he would never marry Simone. The very fact that he could discuss the idea so calmly with himself made the eventuality extremely unlikely.

Noma would be sailing soon — Kim Skene and Midnight Blue had already sailed in scandalous proximity: she would probably forfeit her moving picture contract for this lapse from the moral code — but Noma had not yet succeeded in adding David to her list of temporary lovers. Noma's assiduity reminded Hamish of Donald Bliss's ribald witticism: Why is Noma like a valuable hen? Because she lays a new good egg every day. It had begun to be increasingly evident to Noma, however, that David who had been so easy for some could be the most elusive of men. She may well have to sail, thought Hamish, without accomplishing her purpose.

David, since his return, and Roy's death, had become a somewhat different David, more aloof, more difficult, even more desperate and exasperating in his depravities, but sweeter than usual, more bent on a kind of vague expiation, and certainly more impossible than ever to capture, to surround, to possess. David and Rilda . . . Rilda and David: enigmas. I understand them less than I understand myself, thought Hamish, for the hundredth time, and I don't understand myself at all. They are incomprehensible. Stranger and stranger. Paradoxes. Contradictions.

The sun illumined a gracious picture on Fifth Avenue. At the corner the traffic policeman held up his hand and the black and white cabs, the yellow cabs, the cherry cabs, the green and silver cabs, the Chryslers, the Rolls-Royces, the Fords, and the Packards, lined up restless for the signal to press onward, for all the world like a row of Roman charioteers behind the tape waiting for the race to begin. On the sidewalk pedestrians of every class in every kind of dress of every colour swept past Hamish or walked by his side. The show-windows on this bright spring day were resplendent with temptations for strollers. Hamish was tired of this unaccustomed process of thinking. It was nearly time for luncheon and he had yet to enjoy his first drink. He might, in search of this, visit his club, or any one of the fifty thousand speakeasies with which central New York was honeycombed, depending in his selection on whether he wanted to encounter friends or casual acquaintances or strangers or no one. Donald would still be in his bed: the Wishbone would not yet be open. He refrained from permanently bolting the door until so late in the morning that he could scarcely be expected to open it again until late in the afternoon. Of course, this might be an excellent time to call on the Gräfin. She or Mattie would assuredly offer him a cocktail. Rilda and David might be awake — or would be shortly if David were at home at all. Anyway their bar was always open.

Hello, Hamish.

Although Hamish never felt lonely on the streets of New York, he always felt alone, strange to the crowd, so that he was invariably surprised when some one spoke to him. Now he looked about him without recognizing the source of this salutation.

Hello, Hamish. . . The call was repeated, more distinctly.

This time voice and direction were unmistakable. The voice belonged to King Swan and it came from the kerb. Hamish's eyes following the evidence of his ears, he discovered the chauffeur sitting on the box of his cab with his flag down. Hamish approached him.

Waiting for what Donald calls a desultory dame, King explained. They won't letcher park long neither. Whater you doing?

Nothing, Hamish replied.

Well, that's not news. Sober?

Completely.

Well that *is* news. Want me to take you somewhere? I'll ditch this dame.

Hamish shook his head. Don't want to go anywhere,

he said. He emended this to: I don't know where I want
to go.

King Swan was disappointed. Let me drive you 'round
the Park and back to some bar, he suggested.

Hamish for some inexplicable reason was obstinate.
Thanks, but I don't feel like driving this morning. I want
to toddle.

Waving his hand in farewell to the chauffeur he strolled
on. At Forty-seventh Street he paused to look in a window,
and even as he did so became aware that he was standing
next to some one he knew. He gave the figure a direct
glance and discovered it belonged to Noma. She had not
yet seen him and it was evident that she was so fully pre-
occupied with the display behind the glass that she
might not recognize him. Actually she was the last person
he would have desired to encounter. Yet perversely, he accosted her.

Hamish! You up, and sober?

She was the second person this morning to be astonished
by his condition.

It does seem strange, he admitted. I was just going to
do something about it. Which way are you going?

It doesn't much matter. I was out for a walk.

Automatically, they started to stroll back towards the
Park.

Hamish, you've been rotten to me, was her next comment.

Noma, you know damned well I haven't been anything to you.

That's what I mean, and please don't be an ass. I asked you to help me with David.

What can I do? How can any one help anybody else? Do you want me to tell him that you want him? He already knows that. Do you want me to say, Please be nice to Noma for my sake? He would think I was crazy.

She gave him an oblique glance and smiled. I rather think, she said, you're having me on.

I never was more serious in my life, on the contrary, he responded with some heat.

Hamish, you know perfectly well you could do something. It isn't so much *saying* anything; it's more taking me about with you, so we'd be together more. David is always with you and if I were with you too . . . She smiled her conclusion.

Noma, you are incredible. You and Rosalie and Mrs. Alonzo W. Syreno and . . . are incredible. I don't know what to make of you at all. You seem to believe that David was created merely to give you pleasure. Where does Rilda come in? Where do I come in?

Oh, Rilda! Noma sniffed. Rilda's his wife. And you? You're his best friend. And Rosalie and Mrs. Alonzo W. Syreno? Canailles! Vaches! It's high time you were forgetting these others and yourself and thinking a little more seriously about me. I'm sailing in two weeks and it is my delightful plan to have David sail with me.

He won't.

Then I won't. That's flat.

You must have that man.

I must have that man.

There's music to that.

I know. Let's go up there now, Noma added carelessly.

Up where?

To David's bar, for a drink.

How do you know he'll be there?

If he isn't, you'll get your drink at least.

Rilda . . .

Oh, I can cope with Rilda. Of course, Noma went on impatiently, if you don't want to go with me, it isn't at all necessary. I can go by myself, but you're probably going to take your first drink somewhere and it might as well be there. On the other hand, I don't mind having it look as if you had urged me to accompany you.

You're no end a silly woman and fifty per cent right.

Hamish, if it weren't David, it would be you. I think it will be you next. I very much admire your left ear.

Um. I'll have something to say about that.

Very little. When I make up my mind I'm devastating.

You get what you want.

I do.

You must have that man.

I must have that man. Let's take a taxi. It will be quicker.

Hamish swept the kerb with his eyes and there was King Swan in exactly the same spot where he had left him. So naturally, it was King who drove them to David's.

❊ NINETEEN ❊

David's bar was modern in what Claire Madrilena described as " a nice way." The angles were not too sharp,
the colours were not sombre, and the furniture was not
merely picturesque. The bar-stools of silver and ivory-
white leather were handsome, durable, and comfortable.
The bar of black mirror, bordered with ruby glass, the
walls of alternating panels of yellow and silver, the white
rubber floor with an ultramarine sea-monster laid in the
centre, all appeared at their best in the morning when the
tunnel of graduating glass circles in the ceiling let in
the morning sun. It was David's theory that the morning
sun was about all any human being could put up with,
especially if he were drinking. So along towards three
o'clock all natural light was excluded.

It was nearly one o'clock when Noma and Hamish arrived. Opening the door, Edith explained that neither Rilda
nor David had yet rung and she suggested to the visitors
that they repair to the bar to await their hosts. Further she
offered to provide some one to shake cocktails, should they
require aid.

I feel strong enough this morning to do a little shaking
myself, said Hamish.

In the bar he amused himself by turning over the leaves

251

of a book in which David had written down recipes for cocktails which he, or one of his friends, had invented. Here, for instance, was the Woojums: five parts gin, one part bacardi, a dash of bitters, a dash of absinthe, a teaspoonful of lemon juice, and a little grenadine. On another page he discovered the Hard Daddy: one quarter lemon juice, one quarter maple syrup, and one half whisky. On a third, the Kinkajou: one part grapefruit juice, one part gin, sweetened with honey. Weren't kinkajous honey-bears? So Hamish decided to mix a Martini.

Noma had thrown aside her light cloak and extended herself on the ivory-white leather of the couch when the door was opened slowly and a radiant child appeared.

Good morning, Regent, Hamish greeted him.

Good morning, Uncle Hamish, the child responded gravely.

Regent Westlake was about eight and not very tall for his age. He was a curiously solemn child with a beauty that was almost ethereal. He stood very quietly in the doorway.

Why don't you come in, Regent? Hamish suggested.

Thank you, Uncle Hamish, he replied with dignity. Closing the door carefully behind him, he advanced to the centre of the blue monster in the floor and again halted.

I thought you went to school now, said Hamish.

I do, the child replied, but today I decided not to go.

Something is worrying me very much, Uncle Hamish, he went on diffidently.

My dear Regent, what is it? . . . Hamish was occupied shaking the cocktails.

The boy hesitated before he responded: I wish you could do something about it.

Dear Regent, you must tell me what I am to do something about.

Hamish filled a cocktail glass, drank the contents, and refilled it.

About Rilda and David drinking so much. . . As he blurted this out the child's fingers clutched convulsively at the front of his blouse.

About . . . ! Hamish in his astonishment opened his mouth very wide. . . But why?

Oh, I don't care how much they drink, really, said the child, now more at his ease. It's only I hardly ever see them when they're drinking and I love to see them so much. I s'pose when I'm older and can go to parties myself I won't mind because I can drink with them then, but just now I guess they would stay home more with me if they didn't drink so much.

You uncanny child, you frighten me! Noma, on elbow-supported chin, cried from the couch.

I am sure they would, Hamish gravely assured Regent, and I shall speak to them about it.

Will you, Uncle Hamish? It would be awfully good of

you if you would. . . . The expression on Regent's face was perceptibly brighter. . . . Please remember that when I am a little older and can drink and go to parties myself I won't care what David and Rilda do, but just now it's pretty hard.

Crossing the floor with superb dignity, the boy opened the door and took his departure.

My God, what a kid! cried Noma. He gives me the creeps. He makes me feel like Zaza. Did you ever see that funny old play? There's a scene where the spangled music-hall tart goes to confront her lover's wife, but dissolves in tears and departs at the sight of his child. I hope I shan't be affected in the same way.

His point of view is pretty regular, Hamish remarked. Of course they scarcely ever do see him because they hate to have him see them drunk and they almost always are.

Noma was meditating. I don't believe, she mused, I ever knew before they had a child.

They never talk about him or they always do, Hamish explained lucidly.

Good morning. . . . Simone Fly, very elegant in a black and white tailleur costume, appeared in the doorway.

Morning, Simone, Hamish replied. A little while ago I was wondering why I didn't marry you.

Blaa! Don't be absurd. . . . Smiling broadly, Simone crossed to the bar and examined with interest a bottle of Fiori Alpini with its crystalized edelweiss caught in the golden liqueur the tall bottle contained. . . They do this with roses and carnations in perfume in Spain, she commented. What are you drinking?

Martini? Hamish waved the shaker.

Certainly. Either or.

As Simone mounted a stool, Hamish filled her glass and refilled his own.

Bare-legged, bare-footed David, in a black velvet dressing-gown, drifted in, a bandanna tied around his rebellious curls in lieu of a stocking-cap.

Morning, friends, he cried. Delighted to see you. It's like a gathering of the five nations in the mountains in the dawn. Gimme a drink, Hame.

I don't know about that. I've just had a request to stop your drinking.

And cause a total eclipse of the sun? Who's the reformer?

Regent. He complains, very sweetly, that he never sees you and Rilda because you're always at parties. Wants you to cut out drinking till he's old enough to go out and get drunk with you.

The little beggar! . . . David grinned as he accepted the glass Hamish had filled for him. . . I love him for that. Wants to see us, does he? Well, I call that damned flattering. I don't want to see myself. What's this?

Martini.

You *are* imaginative. Haven't had one for ages, but as

I remember they only contain two kinds of liquor. Let me get in this. I'll mix something potent.

Stepping behind the bar, David began to juggle bottles as if they were Indian clubs.

Where's Rilda? Simone demanded.

Oh, Rilda! Noma cried. It's pleasant to have David alone sometimes.

Do you call this having me alone? David inquired, almost cheerfully. I don't think I've ever been alone in my life. It seems to me my career is as public and as exhausting as that of a stallion — probably more, because a stallion is occasionally locked up in his manger.

You're not complaining surely? Simone asked him.

No, I like it, or else I wouldn't have it. I suppose we all more or less like the way we live or else we'd live the way they do in Pittsburgh or Detroit.

Why don't you sail with me, David? Noma urged him in as insinuating a tone as she could conjure up.

Sail with . . . ? Staring at her in astonishment, David helped himself to another drink.

Yes. We could be quite alone.

David roared with laughter.

There's nothing very subtle about you, Noma. Blaaa! exclaimed Simone.

Sometimes you get what you want by asking for it, Noma retorted.

Sometimes, David echoed enigmatically.

✳ PARTIES ✳

The Gräfin and Freddie appeared in the doorway.

Good morning, everybody, said the little old noble-woman. How nice that sounds, she commented, as she listened to the jingle of the ice in the shaker. What have you put in it this morning, David?

Oh, just ever so much of ever so many things. It's a beautiful morning and I'm very happy to see you all so early and I hope we'll all be plastered before the sun sets.

Let me shake the cocktails, Mr. Westlake. . . Freddie was pleading to be permitted to make himself useful.

They're shaken, son, but you may pass them.

Noma was now sitting upright on the couch. Simone had draped herself around a bar-stool. Hamish was sitting on the bar. David was standing behind the bar. The Gräfin had chosen a comfortable arm-chair. Freddie was passing the tray of cocktails.

I'm going back to London in two weeks, Noma announced, with the air of one preparing the public for an explosion of dynamite.

Hamish groaned. Really, Noma . . .

The door opened and Rosalie Keith appeared.

Rosalie! David was actually surprised. He could not recall that she had ever previously paid him a visit.

I've heard so much about these early morning cocktail parties, she explained, I decided to try one out. Besides one never knows who may be working while one is sleeping.

Looking very mysterious, she joined Simone at the bar.

I suppose Mrs. Alonzo W. Syreno will be the next to turn up, was David's comment, made not without resignation.

Or Malvina Crane, added Noma, not without malice.

David flushed, whistled, and grinned. So you know about that, too? he said.

Again the door opened to admit Rilda, a really lovely Rilda after a good night's rest, in a dressing-gown of silver tissue and chartreuse chiffon which trailed along the floor, a cluster of Claudius Pernet roses in her arms.

Just like the entrance of Tosca, Rilda my dear, cried David. What *are* you going to do with the flowers?

I like yellow roses in the bar, was all that she found to reply.

She nodded good mornings to her guests and arranged the roses in a glass vase she found under the bar.

Well, David, she went on, it could be said that most of your lady friends have come in to pass the time of day.

David grinned sheepishly. Have a cocktail, Rilda, he suggested.

She kissed him.

I should warn you, he continued, that Regent is trying to interfere with our lives. He has gone so far as to request that we give up drinking until he is old enough to get drunk with us.

I know, Rilda, responded, smiling. He was just telling me.

Donald entered with a suitcase.

I thought you might need some cointreau, he said, so I brought you some brandy.

Sidecars! cried David, in ecstasy.

For all I care. Donald appeared resigned. How's General Motors?

Good God, man! David regarded the bootlegger with astonishment. You don't think I've seen the papers yet. Why, it's only just past sunrise. Besides I plunged and lost all. I'm no longer in the market.

It's just like the opening chorus of an opéra-bouffe, Simone remarked, all of us here clinking glasses like villagers on the green.

Somehow it's more like the closing chorus, retorted the Gräfin. I think we're all a little tired.

Dear Adele, what's the matter? Rilda inquired.

Nothing, Rilda. . . The Gräfin smiled through her tears. . . It's the sun and the weather, I think. I must be too happy. . . She wiped her eyes.

Do make some more cocktails, David, Rilda suggested, adding bitterly, There are actually people who believe that because a person is well-fed he has no problems.

David, are you dining with me tonight? Rosalie inquired.

If you like, Rilda responded for her husband. We're getting quite accustomed to it and our cook loves it. Please have soft roe, gaspacho, and yose nabe.

✳ PARTIES ✳

It seems to me that you and David are frightfully polite to each other today, was Simone's comment.

That's the danger signal, Rilda explained. It probably means we've agreed to separate.

Agreed to separate! Noma and Rosalie cried together in enthusiastic surprise.

My dear ladies, said David, it means nothing of the kind. It means that Hamish and I will get drunk as usual this afternoon, and that we shall somehow manage to arrive at Rosalie's in time for dinner where, of course, we shall meet Rilda and that, despite the fact we have purchased tickets to see Zimbule O'Grady in Buttered Toast, we shall spend most of the evening at Donald's and probably end up in Harlem. That is the life of our times in words of two syllables. I am not bitter about it. I accept it as the best we can do.

But . . . cried an exasperated Noma.

Exactly! David interrupted her. That's just what I say about it. We're here because we're here, and we should be extremely silly not to make the worst of it.

As he raised his glass, they all lifted theirs.

Ha! Ha! The Gräfin was chuckling, her face broken into a thousand wrinkles. It is so funny, David, so very funny, and I love your country.

April 22, 1930
New York

CARL VAN VECHTEN

Born in 1880 in Cedar Rapids, Iowa, Carl Van Vechten graduated from the University of Chicago and went to work at the *Chicago American* reporting "Gossip of the Chicago Smart Set." His prose, as his biographer Bruce Kellner has described it, was "beset with frappés and doilies," the style of some of his later comic novels. He was fired from the paper in 1906 for, as Van Vechten expressed it, "lowering the tone of the Hearst papers."

From Chicago he moved to New York, becoming, first, the assistant music critic for the *New York Times* and, later, the drama critic for the *New York Press,* to which Djuna Barnes also contributed. Traveling over the next two decades between Paris and New York, Van Vechten wrote seven volumes of literary and musical criticism, and several novels, including the roman à clef *Peter Whiffle* (1922), *The Blind Bow-Boy* (1923), *The Tattooed Countess* (1924), *Red* (1925), *Firecrackers* (1925), *Nigger Heaven* (1926), and *Spider Boy* (1928).

Parties, published originally in 1930, concerns, as do others of his books, the Harlem community, which during this period was experiencing a renaissance in literature, theater, music, and dance. Van Vechten had been one of the major figures in introducing the white community to this Harlem, and he would have close ties to Harlem figures throughout his life, photographing and writing about Paul Robeson, Count Basie, James Weldon Johnson, Billie Holiday, and many others. A collection of some of his famed photographs was recently published.

A long-time friend of Gertrude Stein, Van Vechten served as general editor for the Yale editions of the writings of Gertrude Stein published in the 1950s. Van Vechten continued photographing until his death in 1964.

SUN & MOON CLASSICS

Sun & Moon Classics is a publicly supported nonprofit program to publish new editions and translations or republications of outstanding world literature of the late-nineteenth and twentieth centuries. Through its publication of living authors as well as great masters of the century, the series attempts to redefine what usually is meant by the idea of a "classic" by dehistorizing the concept and embracing a new, ever-changing literary canon.

Organized by The Contemporary Arts Educational Project, Inc., a nonprofit corporation, and published by its program, Sun & Moon Press, the series is made possible, in part, by grants and individual contributions.

This book was made possible, in part, through a matching grant from the National Endowment for the Arts, from the California Arts Council, through an organizational grant from the Andrew W. Mellon Foundation, and through contributions from the following individuals.

Charles Altieri (Seattle, Washington)
John Arden (Galway, Ireland)
Dennis Barone (West Hartford, Connecticut)
Jonathan Baumbach (Brooklyn, New York)
Bill Berkson (Bolinas, California)
Steve Benson (Berkeley, California)
Sherry Bernstein (New York, New York)
Bill Corbett (Boston, Massachusetts)
Robert Crosson (Los Angeles, California)
Tina Darragh and P. Inman (Greenbelt, Maryland)
Fielding Dawson (New York, New York)
Christopher Dewdney (Toronto, Canada)
In Memoriam: Philip Dunne
George Economou (Norman, Oklahoma)
Elaine Equi and Jerome Sala (New York, New York)
Richard Elman (Stonybrook, New York)
Lawrence Ferlinghetti (San Francisco, California)
Richard Foreman (New York, New York)
Howard N. Fox (Los Angeles, California)
Jerry Fox (Aventura, Florida)
In Memoriam: Rose Fox
Melvyn Freilicher (San Diego, California)
Peter Glassgold (Brooklyn, New York)
Perla and Amiram V. Karney (Bel Air, California)
Fred Haines (Los Angeles, California)

BOOKS IN THE SUN & MOON CLASSICS SERIES

*First edition
** Revised edition